To The

GW00692302

RRRA....

Paul Eccentric is a poet, novelist, singer, lyricist, playwright and director. He is the Artistic Director of the RRRANTS Collective and coaches aspiring performers in the art of stage confidence. Among his various musical forays into the worlds of jazz, punk, polka, skiffle, swing and doowop he has both written and sung for The Odd Eccentric, The Senti-Mentals and Sly Quip & The Quick Wits. His most recent albums 'Two Heads', 'Who Knows, Who Cares' and 'Odds'n Sods' are available to download from iTunes. He has published two poetry collections 'Lyrical Quibble & Quip' and 'The Kult Of The Kazoo', a novel 'Down Among The Ordinaries', and a self-help guide: 'Quaking In Me Stackheels'. As the mouthy half of beatranters The Antipoet he has published four collections of beat poetry: 'Tights Not Stockings', 'Hanging With Poets', 'Random Words' and 'Ere's One For The Kiddies'. The first three series of RRRANTANORY Little Stories have been published on CD, with series 4-6 following in 2013.

[signature] Aug 20

PLEASE RETURN TO
THE BOX WHEN READ

Other titles from www.deserthearts.com:

RRRANTANORY
Little Stories
by
Paul Eccentric

. . . a selection of stories from the RRRANTS Radio production: 'RRRANTANORY Little Stories' originally broadcast on MyWordRadio.com from October 2011, imagined by Paul Eccentric and realised by Beef Grant. Cover illustration and design by Mark Gordon. Edited by Nick Awde.

DESERT ♥ HEARTS

Paul Eccentric can be contacted for lectures,
workshops, schools and one-to-one tutoring
through: **donna@rrrants.com**
www.rrrants.com ♦ **www.pauleccentric.co.uk**

First published in 2013
by
Desert♥Hearts
www.deserthearts.com

PO BOX 2131
London W1A 5SU
England

ISBN 978 1 908755 07 0

Printed & bound by
Marston, Abindgon, United Kingom

In memory of
Hazel Brown
(1928-2013)

'The Pedestrians' and *'Someone Else Completely'*
were first published as part of the
'Out of The Frying Pan' series
for Jokat Audio in 2003

Contents

Author's note

*The following collection of short stories were written
to be read aloud as part of my 2011 MyWordRadio.
com series
'RRRANTANORY Little Stories' and at my live RRRANTANORY
readings, held monthly at The Teabox, Richmond, England since
April 2012 and at Coco, Croxley Green, Herts, England,
hence, what some may feel, my excessive use of
contractions, subclauses, apparently lazy
grammar and narrative asides.*

http://www.facebook.com/rantanory.littlestories

*If in doubt,
find yourself an audience
and read it out!*

—Paul Eccentric, Spring 2013

*This book is dedicated to Beef Grant, without whose time,
patience and technological wizardry the RRRANTANORY series
would not have existed, and to Jemma & Mike at The Teabox without
whose teashop, the bulk of these stories would never have been written;
to Nick Awde for his faith and backing; and, as always,
to Donna for her eternal unflinching support
of every daft idea I come up with.*

1

The
Pedestrians

'Course they're all dead now.'

'Murder?'

Well now hold on a minute. Let's not be hasty. Have you never heard of extenuating circumstances?

From the beginning?

Well . . . I don't know. Where did it start? Like anything else, I suppose. One thing leads to another, you know. You don't think about things starting at the time, you only see that later, in retrospect. You see, they were always there. Even before I knew them, I was aware of them. I must have seen them even then, just glimpsed them out of the corner of my eye. Like road signs on a route that you travel every day. You know they're there, but you don't actually see them every time you pass them. You wouldn't notice if they suddenly weren't there. Furniture? Yeah, that's probably a good analogy. They were just a part of the background scenery. They'd have had to be bouncing off my bonnet for me to have noticed them. When did I first see them? You mean actually see them, don't you? Recognise them, realise that I knew them, yeah?

Well . . . I suppose it would have to have been the time when the captain got hit by the airport express. I saw him go down. First time I'd seen him without his cap—I'd never thought of him as a baldie before. Odd, really.

But that was the first thing that struck me. There he was sprawled across by the bypass in a tangle of splattered fruit and veg and I all could think about was 'where's his hair?' I'd kind of built up a picture of him in my mind, standing on deck behind one of those big steering-wheels, one hand guiding the boat, the other holding a brass telescope to his one good eye.

Did he? Did he really? Well that just shows you how much I hadn't noticed him, doesn't it. Two eyes, you say. Ha! So no eyepatch, then. Hmm. Suppose not. That would be silly. No, I know that now. But he did look like a captain, didn't he? He had that weatherbeaten, leathered skin look—and the beard. You must have noticed the beard?

He lived on one of those old houseboats down on the canal. Well no. I know he doesn't actually live there, I know that now, but at the time, the time of his accident, that's where I thought he lived and that was where I thought he was going. Yes, that was what I told the police. I didn't know his name at the time, but I'd seen him about so often that I felt I knew him. I was only trying to help.

And the librarian?

Well, again, I always passed him in the same spot on the same day. Very punctual he was. No more than five minutes walk from the library, and only seven minutes before opening up time. Give him a minute to unlock, switch off the alarm and collect the post, a minute to hang his duffel coat and his bag in the cloakroom and he's ready to serve.

No, that wasn't the only reason I thought he was a librarian. I told you. I never really looked at these people, I just kind of took them in—you know, subliminally. He had this hair, almost to his belt. Wiry, smelly and grey. He tied it back in a ponytail. And a beard. Yes another beardie. But unlike the captain's muffler, this one was like . . . Jesus. And he wore clogs as well. Wooden clogs. Tie-dye T-shirts in the summer and a scarf like Doctor Who's in winter. What else could he have been? What other job would've employed him?

No. But then I never went in the library, did I? He played the guitar too. No, I never actually heard him play it . . . but it was obvious wasn't it?

I always wanted to be able to play the guitar. I thought maybe he might teach me. Her? You mean the witch? Nah, I never liked her. I didn't like that look she always gave me. That supercilious: 'I've got your number' look. Contemptuous. Like she held me personally responsible for her life of pain and misery.

Yeah. She noticed me alright. No, she never spoke to me. She didn't have to. That dismissive sneer of hers said it all. She had a flat somewhere, a council flat. I was paying for it, of course—well, we all are really. She liked that. It was a kind of punishment for all these things she thought I'd done to her. She pulled out in front of me on that rusty old bike of hers. That's right, the one with the wicker basket and the kiddie seat, no indication, she just looked at me. Like she was putting a hex on me. Like I'm supposed to just realise the extent of her powers and just let her in!

No. Emphatically no! I do not hate women! I only followed her because . . . well you know why I followed her! For the same reason I followed the assassin.

Well, no, of course they didn't find a gun. He's a professional! He may have fooled you, but remember—I saw him every day. I notice things. That nonchalance—it was just a façade! He was furtive. Yeah. That's what struck me about the assassin. He thought he was a master of disguise, thought he could just blend into the crowd, but I had his number! He always wore just the right things and they were always new, but I've seen plainclothes policemen looking more natural. A classical musician?

You know your problem, don't you? You're too damn trusting! No, that's what we're supposed to think. That was his cover. It was the classic double-bluff.

There was no Strad in that box, y'know.

Well, no. I didn't see his gun either, I told you, this bloke's good! I mean, how many self respecting hitmen walk around with an Uzi inside a violin case these days? I expect it's all done with mirrors.

Hate them? No I didn't hate them. I looked upon them as my friends. Well, except for the witch. I didn't like the witch. I even felt sorry for some of them. Hmm? Well the roadie for a start. Poor guy. He just looked so aimless. But you can see it in his eyes. I've got a sixth sense for that stuff, you know. I see someone and I just know where they've been, what they've done—who they are. The roadie had really lived. In the seventies. He'd been into everything. He was a real pleasure-seeker. Then one day he just took too much. He woke up late and the circus had left town. They'd gone without him. All he had were the clothes he stood up in. So he sobered up there and then. He's spent the last thirty years waiting for them to come back. Poor guy. Ready-meal dinners for one. He lost his mind. He couldn't quite believe they'd do that to him. He still wears that same tour shirt. He's got the same haircut and cut-off denim jacket. I feel for him. They're never coming back, you know. The band split up in '74. Nobody told him.

Nobody made me follow them. They intrigued me. I saw these people on a daily basis, like I said. I felt I'd got to know them. You know, like they were old friends. I waved to the captain the next time I saw him—was a while later, mind. He had a bit of a limp by then. Ha! I dunno, I think they might've taken his leg off, given him a wooden one. Yeah, I waved at him. I tooted and waved. And you know what he did? Two-fingered salute, that's what!

I don't know. Did he recognise me from the incident? Maybe I just shook him up with my airhorn. Who can tell? So you've said. So they said at the time, but I suppose that's why I decided to follow him. I wanted to explain. I hadn't run him over. I'd helped pick him up! And I'd told the police everything I knew.

Well who was to say? He could have been lying. Maybe he hasn't got a mooring licence, maybe he smuggles stuff. I don't know why he gave them a false identity. So I followed him. I didn't stalk him like the papers said. I just followed him one day, to see where he went.

I was practically a mate! I saw him every day of the week, had done for longer than I could remember.

No, I didn't know his name!

Is it relevant?

I followed him home. I just wanted to see where he lived. That was all.

Nothing sinister. I didn't break in, no.

He didn't invite me in either.

I sort of . . . *fell* in, I suppose. No, I didn't hit him, I *blocked* him.

Yes. That was when he hit his head, yeah.

I caught him as he fell, sort of, overbalanced and found myself inside.

I didn't take anything. Yeah. I had a bit of a look round. Just tat, really, bric-a-brac. A bit chintzy. Not the sort of stuff I'd expect of a sailor. No, I didn't report it to the police. Well, I hadn't realised he was . . . you know. I thought he'd just knocked himself out. Well, because he was a liar, wasn't he. He'd have blamed me! He already had them convinced he was a retired chemist!

And the librarian?

Hmm. Well that was just stupid. I asked him to teach me to play the guitar. He didn't have to react like that. We were mates. Well . . . sort of. No, I didn't know his name!

He was a civil engineer? Well I don't know how well that pays, but he looked like he could have done with a bit of extra cash. I was offering to pay him. I know he said I was trying to mug him but I offered him money. He could've just said no. He didn't have to swing that bloody rope bag at me. No, he fell. It was those clogs of his. He'd have made it to the other side if it hadn't been for those stupid wooden shoes. No, I don't think he saw the lorry. Wouldn't have made much difference if he had.

Alright, so maybe the witch was deliberate. She was always doing it, stepping out on crossings or pulling out in front of me on that bloody old bike! It wasn't murder. I hadn't planned to run her over. She just didn't look where she was going. Alright, well I'll admit I might've made a slight miscalculation when I tried to pay the assassin to kill the roadie. I'm not a killer, alright! I just wanted to help him, to put him out of his misery. No, look!

You've asked me that before and I told you then. I'm not a serial killer. There's no link between these people. They were just always there. They got on my nerves!

They were just . . . pedestrians.

2

Random Selection

Fleur had been perfectly content. She had a job that she absolutely loved, two completely distinct social circles: the girls from the salon and her old mates from school, and for the last six months had been sharing a ground-floor flat on the edge of a 'newbuild development complex' with her apprentice footballer boyfriend, Brian.

She was proud to have achieved so much more in her first twenty years than her parents had achieved in forty. Brian even had a car, and as a step up from her mother's high-rise window box, they had a slabbed area beside their front door with four large pots on it that she and Brian liked to call their garden.

When she wasn't out clubbing with Brian or her mates, Fleur liked to watch the television. She followed her soaps religiously, gobbling up the intricacies of the character's fictional lives with the same zealous fervour with which she so completely devoured her other great passion: the celebrity gossip magazines. She was a great reader. Not much got past Fleur. She had her finger on the pulse, she knew how it all knitted together, she knew what life was all about and she loved nothing more than to yack endlessly to anybody who stood close enough to her for long enough about who was doing what to whom behind whose back.

Fleur knew where she stood. She knew what was going on in

the world. She knew exactly what to buy and where to buy it from because the adverts kept her up to date.

But she didn't know everything. She didn't know all the boring stuff that happened to other people whom she didn't know and who led weird lives in countries that she couldn't point to on a map and who didn't have television or magazines. She didn't read those bits in her newspaper, she just stuck to the important bits. And the adverts. She did like her adverts.

The adverts gave her mind a chance to catch its breath between ideas.

One of the things that Fleur didn't know about was the existence of aliens, and so when she got abducted by one whilst walking home from the salon one night, she found herself utterly flummoxed and, for once, completely lost for words.

The aliens in question had been attracted to Earth after unexpectedly picking up a series of random transmissions as they coasted past the outer planets of the solar system on their way to a party. Curious, as their galactic satnav seemed convinced that there was no sentient life on any of the ten planets of this system, they chose a continent and a life sign at random and sent down a transmat beam to extract it. The transmissions that had been beaming out into space had been quite unintelligible, even after their translation software had converted the squall into standard, leading the visitors to presume that a society must have evolved here so cut off from the rest of civilization that it could have developed an entirely unique technology.

Fleur woke up to find herself naked and strapped spreadeagled to a table with two huge catlike things in spangly suits staring down at her. They shot questions at her like her friend Marnie did on a Tuesday morning if she'd missed the previous evenings edition of the soaps. They spoke fairly good English for cats, she thought, but she hadn't a clue what they were going on about. It was all 'socio-politico' this and 'eco-techno' that—none of which she knew anything about. Eventually they showed her what they said were some random transmissions that they had picked up from space and asked if she could interpret them. *Could she??* So she filled them in on the last ten years worth of soap storylines, reality shows and advertising campaigns as they stood silently above her. When she had finished they returned her clothes in silence and set her back down where they found her.

As they left the system they dropped a marker buoy into orbit as a warning to other shortcutters that the planet below was some kind of long-lost asylum colony that should be avoided at all costs for the sake of sanity.

Fleur, on the other hand, put the whole experience down to a spiked Bacardi Breezer.

3
Painting
the Town

They'd put him at the back of the class and given him a pair of blunt-edged scissors and a pot of glitter. Ooh, sparkly colours! They'd told him not to eat the glue or to stick it in his eyes and not to go over the clearly defined edges. 'No, don't go over the edges, Larry, that's important. You gotta stay within the lines. If you don't learn anything else today, Larry, then at least you ought to be able to understand that.'

'This is how you do it, Larry, this is how it must be done,' said the foreman. 'Follow the marks we've put down for you and just paint from here to here. Yes, it all has to be white and no, you can't put a flourish on the end. You're not an artist, Larry, you're a painter. You need to be clear and precise. People like precision. People need precision.'

But Larry didn't like precision. And Larry didn't like lines. Always with the bloody lines! What was wrong with these people? There was nothing natural about straight lines, they were an entirely human conceit. The only nod toward straightness that nature had ever conceded was the hazy horizon, and as any rainbow-chaser worth his reputation knows, the horizon is as much an optical illusion as the cerulean appearance of the sky and the sea that meet to form it.

They all thought he was stupid.

People always had done. They had mistaken individuality for idiocy again.

It was often the way. He had been educated 'secondary modern' during the seventies, long before the term 'political correctness' and all deference to it had even been thought up. The teachers had noticed that Larry had been different to the other children, but back then had had neither the training nor the inclination to understand, diagnose or deal with his various 'difficulties', so they had stuck him in a class full of tomorrow's muggers and murderers and left him to get on with it. The other kids had been no better. They had also noticed his 'monginess' and in time-honoured fashion had dealt with it as they had observed their parents dealing with 'different people' by renaming him 'Spazz' and 'Twitchy Larry'.

If there had been a scientific name back then for what would later be called his 'condition', then the people around him had been blissfully oblivious to it, so his peers' insensitive nicknames had stuck with him, etched into his soul like indelible tattoos along with his flimsy grip on self-worth and his negative self-esteem, trapping him in an Ouroboros cycle of can't do/won't do which had only worked to reinforce everybody's stultifying opinions of his likely abilities.

Larry closed his eyes and took a long, deep breath in, holding for a count of twenty before slowly releasing in a carefully measured flow.

He repeated the exercise twice more, not because anybody had ever shown him how to 'centre' himself in the face of a stressful situation, but because he had perceived a need to achieve a state of serenity and so had worked it out for himself. He was good at working things out for himself. So long as people left him to it, Larry had discovered that there was actually very little that he couldn't do. He hadn't wanted to take this job, though. What he had really wanted to have been was a tattooist, that would have been a profession that he had just known he could have excelled in. That had been his dream, but he had been aware of the limitations that his 'disability' imposed and the levels of self-control that he would have required for that were still at this point some way beyond him. He opened his eyes, put his hands on his trolley and walked forward, his index finger depressing the paint-release trigger and allowing the mechanism to deploy a smooth line of quick-drying brilliant white paint to the tarmac beneath. He counted to five inside his head and then released the trigger and let go of the trolley, stepping back in a fluid movement before spasming involuntarily, his arms jerking wildly as if he had just received a fatal dose of electricity. Recomposing himself almost instantly, Twitchy Larry stepped back up to the plate and repeated the process of relining the sliproad to the motorway, stopping as necessary between lines to assert himself.

It was similar to tattooing, he thought, mistakes were just as difficult to remove, but where was the artistry in road lining?

And why did it all have to be so bloody repetitive? If only they would let him paint the cycles on the cycle lanes. Even that would have been better than those constant white lines. His only deviation came in the summer months when, twice per season, they let him loose in the park to mark out the football pitches. Oh, what fun. Curved lines!

Over the years Larry had learned to control his violent spasms in his off hours. He had been tested. There was nothing neurologically amiss. Every habitual tic and jerk could be put down to nerves, apparently.

It was the stress of having to follow other people's patterns that brought them on, patterns and orders that did not sit comfortably with the way that his mind worked.

Perhaps it was his brain's way of telling him to lead and not to follow? If they would just leave him alone and let him do it his way then he just knew that he could've been the Picasso of road-liners! He'd already achieved so much more than had ever been expected of him. He had found ways of doing things that nobody else had, ordinary day-to-day tasks that had seemed insurmountable when he had been at school. And his way had often been better than the way that they had told him was the 'Right Way'.

In fact, he had often considered whether it wasn't actually him that was the spack after all, but all those so-called 'normal' people who followed the 'Right Way' just because they couldn't think of anything better to do. Yeah. That was more the case! He was something more than they were, not less!

So that night Larry went back to the depot after dark. He loaded up the liner's truck, (the one that they had never trusted him to drive) with as much paint as its vats would take and set off into town. It was a shame that road paint only came in two colours—the white that he normally used and dayglo yellow for painting the parking restrictions—but it would have to do. He started on the high street.

Where there had traditionally been a pair of unbroken white 'no overtaking' lines down the centre of the carriageway, complemented by a pair of double yellows just off the kerb on either side, Larry painted a series of white-stalked daffodils.

When he reached the junction with St Kitts Street, where normally one would have expected to have seen a demarcation of double staggered lines, Larry painted a hula girl and an eight-foot parrot. Where the roundabout should have been there now sat an intricately detailed yellow and white Spanish galleon. He signed all of his paintings 'Twitch' before moving on to another road and redesigning its standard lineage with a classic tattoo motif.

He ran out of paint just before dawn but it didn't matter. He had made his point. He returned the truck to the depot and then climbed up onto the roof to sit back and watch the normal people come to terms with a little bit of anarchic thinking.

There were a lot of casualties.

Normal people aren't used to having to consider their responses at road junctions. They've always just followed what the lines have told them to do. What was the correct procedure for approaching a giant golden eagle? Or the four horsemen of the apocalypse? Does one give way to the right or is it first come first served when you see a bloody great ship's anchor with the legend 'mum 'n' dad' on a scroll beneath it?

He hadn't wanted to see people getting hurt, but he supposed it had been an inevitable consequence. It was their own fault, really. They should have learned to think for themselves when they'd had the chance. He doubted that they would understand the statement that he had been making, that he had been freeing them from their bonds and offering them a less monotonous approach to road use. Nobody would ever fall asleep at the wheel again! It was genius!

Prison, Larry discovered, is also full of straight lines.

4

Someone Else Completely

Are you happy with who you are? Have you ever wanted to be someone else completely? Have you ever seen anybody else whom you'd rather be? Have you ever tried to be someone else? Do you think it's possible to change? Do you believe that people do change over the course of lifetime?

Fundamentally, I mean. Anyone can change their look, their style of their comportment. That's easy. That's just a mask anyway. You do that all the time. You don't even realise you're doing it. Fashions come, fashions go and you think you're so aloof. You don't think you're being affected by the whimsicalities of twenty first century culture, until you look back at a photograph of yourself taken five years ago and you see . . . that you've changed.

Maybe only subtly, but you're a different person to whom you used to be. That haircut that you thought so 'classic', so out-of-time. God, that you could have left the house looking like that!

It's not always conscious, you see. It just happens. You're in tune somehow with the world around you. There's a whole area of the brain that's devoted to absorbing the mood of the moment and gauging your stylistic response accordingly. It's a self-preservation reflex that works on the same principle as acute change in accent for the relocated.

You can't fight it. It's viral. It's in the air. It's called progress and progress equates with a better standard of living. Anybody who tries to stand in the way of the speeding juggernaut of progress is likely to end up as retro roadkill in the gutter of evolution. You have to adapt to survive.

But what of opinion and affiliation? Do you think it's possible to go to bed a Socialist and wake up a Tory? Of course it is. It happens every day. You put it down to enlightenment, say you saw it in a dream. You blame subliminal advertising or biased education for you latter day revelation. But however you excuse your mutinous defections, loath as you may be to accept the inevitable, you change.

But what about us? The real us. Do you think it's possible to change your personality, your psyche, your ID, just like you'd change your shoes?

I once heard a psychiatrist say that there are only two ways to change your personality. The first would be an intensive course of psychotherapy, held daily over a twenty-year period. The second would involve a severe bump on the head.

Well I've had my share of blows to the head, quite a number of which were self-inflicted in an attempt to prove this theory, and I can honestly say that I've never noticed one iota of change to the way I see the world. So what is it that makes us who we are?

Is it nurture? Is it continued exposure to the ingrained habits of our forebears, patterns that were imprinted on us at a malleable age, creating the hybrid of characteristics that control us like some imaginary demon driver sitting behind our eyes, steering us through our lives with no thought for free will or self-doubt?

Or is it nature? Are we simply the result of a genetic lottery a bit from here, a bit from there, some unbreakable programme instilled in us at conception and with us until the lights go out on our own personal quests?

Who am I to say? And who *am* I to say? Me: the unchanging man. I watch them from my window, going about their daily lives.

I watch them change from day to day as they process influence from the evolving world around them, making new decisions based on the stimuli that they come into contact with.

But I don't change. I am who I am, I am who I've always been. I want to change, so help me, I want to change. I want to be like those people down there, but I'm not.

I'm your proverbial square peg. I'm their milky curdle floating in their stewed tea. I'm the fly in their ointment. I don't fit in. I never have done. I've always been the odd one out, the one the world didn't seem to effect. I'm immune to change, or so it would seem.

But it's worse than that. My failure to blend in with my surroundings, to be a part of this ever mutating community has made me into some kind of catalyst for change. Ironic, isn't it? I have the curious ability to be able to alter the mood of any gathering I attend. Heads used to turn whenever I entered a room, conversational emphasis would shift at my presence. It used to make me feel important. Well it should, shouldn't it? Having people you don't even know talk about you as you pass, noticing their stares from across the street. It's an honour usually reserved for the trendsetter, that charismatic entrepreneur that your ovine Joe Bloggs feels so compelled to emulate. Yet here they were noticing me! I quite got off on it for a while, I don't mind telling you, until it started to hurt. I didn't want to be different, you see, I wasn't trying to stand out. I was missing something. If there's a gene that helps you fit, then I'm lacking it. We all want to feel a part of things sometimes, don't we? Even Screaming Lord Sutch: a man who always set himself up as an eccentric, a unique individual. A collective of like-minded eccentrics. The Monster Raving Loony Party. Non-fitters with something to fit into.

I had begun to matter and I didn't want to matter. I didn't want to affect things.

And then one day a terrible thing happened that would change the world forever. I've tried to rationalise that it wasn't my fault, that the driver of the airport express should have been paying more attention to the road than he was to me. If he had been, then he might have seen that old gentleman before he bounced off his windshield and tragedy could have been averted.

I know I shouldn't feel guilty. I know it wasn't my fault directly. Nobody blamed me . . . openly.

But if I hadn't been there at that precise moment, if I had been somewhere else or someone else completely, then things might have been different. The world would have kept to its original course. The web of life was altered that day and who will ever know how drastically? What great invention might that old man been about to unveil? Who would not now be rescued by him from a burning building? And what great strides towards world peace would not now be broached?

Everything had changed and I had changed it.

So I took myself out of the equation, I resolved not to be a part of things at all. For if I didn't interact with the world, how could I affect it?

Now I'm just a voyeur. I sit here on the third floor watching it all go by. I'm not a recluse nor an agoraphobic. I do still have to venture forth for supplies. But I'm careful, see. I wait until everybody else has gone to bed. Of course, I have to tailor my needs to what's on offer at the all-night garage, but it's a sacrifice worth taking. They know me there and they don't take any unnecessary chances. They don't even open the door to let me in, which is a blessing. They feed me my purchases beneath a bulletproof glass shield. I like that. No risk. The only drawback to my non-involvement policy is the rubbish. I daren't throw anything away. I keep it all in here with me. I couldn't bear for someone to trip over my waste or allow it to foul the ecosystem for others. I wouldn't want to think that I had contributed to the destruction of the ozone layer or anything like that. How would I sleep at night?

So it's getting pretty crowded in here now. I know I've got a television somewhere, but I haven't seen it for years. At least I don't have to vacuum any more, on account that I can't see the carpet. And that's probably a good thing too, because the noise always used to annoy the neighbours, which made them cross, which meant that they went to work cross and as a result probably ruined a lot of other people's lives in return. All of which could have been traced back to me.

So I keep myself to myself. I don't rock the boat, as it were. It's a lonely life, keeping out of everybody's way, but I keep myself going by watching from my window. I can see a lot from up here. You'd probably be surprised at just what does go on during the course of a single day right outside your own home.

Did you know, for instance, that Mrs Fenton is having an illicit affair on Wednesday afternoons with Mr Puri from the paper shop? I don't suppose you did. They're very careful. You'd have to be extremely diligent to notice. And Mr and Mrs Batts? Did you know that they are one and the same person? Have you ever wondered why they're never seen out together?

Oh you get to see it all from here. I know who robbed mad Mr Vartes last Christmas. And it wasn't who you'd expect. I'm not going to tell you though. I'm not going to get involved. I keep schtum. Just like yesterday when poor Mr Stevens got mugged, right outside my door. Horrible business that was, I can see his wife down there now, sellotaping flowers to the lamp-post where he died. Such a shock for everybody. And all for fifty quid and a fake Rolex watch.

Now that one would really surprise you. It sure as hell surprised me. And in broad daylight too. You'd have thought that somebody would have seen something, but the police say they've nothing to go on. No witnesses. Well, except for one.

Best not to get involved, though, eh?

Best not to change the status quo. I'm not a part of that world any more. I only watch.

I'm someone else completely.

5

Miserable Old Sod

Alf Burrage was a miserable sod. He always had been. It was his defining characteristic. You could, if you felt so inclined, spend some time speculating the whys and the wherefores of his singular disposition. You could, perhaps, if you felt the need to offer him the benefit of a fair trial, delve into his obviously troubled psyche in search of some kind of retributional validation for his utterly joyless daily demeanour and, maybe, you never know, you might even get lucky and unearth the cataclysmic catalyst that had sparked his terminal dissatisfaction with the world that he hated so much. You could, that was, if you cared enough about him to bother. But why should you? He had never displayed any obvious sign of any inner human quality or redeeming features that might have suggested that he was anything other than that which he appeared to be. He was, as I've already told you, a miserable sod.

Am I being mean? Is it justified to name and shame in this manner, to expect you merely to take my word for the fact that Alf was not a many-faceted human being like the rest of us, but instead just the living embodiment of a lazy epitaph? No, probably not. So why don't you try living next door to him for thirty years and seeing for yourself, then, hmm?

Alf had never been an easy man to know. If your interaction with him were to occur on a good day, that was, a day when nothing particular had yet to incite his disproportionately venomous wrath, then the best that you could've hoped for would have been a sanctimonious sneer in your general direction or a grunt and a thwack from his stick. But reactions like this were a rarity to be savoured. I long ago lost count of the number of bricks and bottles and on one occasion a handgrenade, that had been thrown at or through my windows as his preferred method of letting me know that he had heard me mowing my lawn, starting my car or flushing my toilet after 9pm. The grenade wasn't live, of course, the firing mechanism had been removed, according to the bomb squad. He wasn't quite that bad! He may not have had that much respect for other life forms, but I had always hoped that he would draw the line at actual murder.

Alf hated a lot of things, but nothing more so than cats. I don't know why! Why don't you ask him? In all the years I've had the misfortune to know him, I've never actually had a two-sided conversation with the man, that is, a conversation in which I get to join in. Please let me know if you find out, if you decide to give him that liberal 'benefit of the doubt' by looking into his background. Perhaps he was mauled as a child? Or maybe his parents were eaten by a tiger on a day out at Windsor Safari Park? I neither know nor care. You'll find that you tend to worry less about a madman's motives when you share a party wall with one.

He really didn't like cats, though. He detested seagulls and he despised pigeons and he held a particular dislike of pizza leaflet distributors, but he saved his particular brand of Alf Burrage trademark ire for the common or garden cat.

Me, I can take em or leave 'em, I've never owned one but I'd never have hurt one. Yes, they can be a bit of a nuisance, digging up your favourite flowerbed to lay a cable and ripping open your bins to get to your leftovers, and to be fair, the cats around here did seem to be a little more organised than I would have said was strictly natural and I had often wondered if they did actually set out to taunt Alf, possibly for the exercise or maybe in some kind of elaborate revenge for crimes committed against their kin. And even if that was the case, then they would have been on a hiding to nothing as Alf had just declared war on feline kind with the acquisition of a shotgun, two revolvers and enough ammunition to stage a fairly accurate recreation of the St Valentine's Day Massacre.

Alf was sat on what passed for his patio, khaki cap on head, shotgun across his lap, playing with a jagged-edged gutting knife like a second-rate Bond henchman waiting for his scene. There were going to be no prisoners taken that day. As I watched from my window vantage-point I spotted Scab, the squatter's cat from over the back fence. Cheerful little chap was Scab, treated all humans that he passed as long-lost friends in what was quite possibly a tried and tested routine which no doubt more often than not bore fruit or titbits of some kind. I had seen him before Alf had, obscured as he was to all but somebody watching him from this angle, by the rusting hulk of Alf's old petrol mower. Scab wasn't expecting trouble. There was nothing furtive about his entrance through the wonky panel. He must have known that Alf was not a potential food source, and that trespass on this side of the fence was likely to be met with extreme, if not entirely accurate force, but he didn't seem at all wary as he positioned himself with his back to the house on the top of the long abandoned compost heap and prepared to divulge himself of his morning burden.

From that distance Alf could quite easily have planted a pellet in the spent oilcan right next to the cat, quite literally scaring the shit out of him. But he must have decided that the shot was too easy as he rejected the single-shot rifle in favour of his two six-shooters. He was on top of the poor moggy before Scab had even heard him coming. The first shot caught him right in the arse, causing Scab to enact a perfect pitch Wyle E Coyote impression before landing face down in the scrub. The second, third, fourth, fifth and six shots that peppered his scraggy body ensured that his final movements were spasmodic and involuntary.

I choked as I watched this. I couldn't quite believe what I was witnessing and made a mental note never to flush the chain during the night again. I'd known Alf Burrage for a long time. He'd always been a nasty piece of work. He'd always been a miserable sod. He had terrorised the street for three decades with his unfathomably vindictive attitude. He had been a total bastard to the local wildlife. But this . . . this had changed everything for me. The look on his face as he poked poor Scab's lifeless body with his boot was one of unadulterated ecstasy. He had crossed a line that day from which I couldn't see a way back.

I heard a scrabbling sound of nails on brick and swung my binoculars to cover this new distraction. It was Mouse, by the look of it, the Batts' portly moggy, trying to climb into my garden over the wall that separated me on the detached side from the alleyway, but struggling to hoist his belly onto the top. He meowed, either in pain, panic or frustration, I couldn't decide which, as his extended claws grappled with the pointing and he began to slip backwards. I wanted to warn him, even though he was most likely only visiting me to do his business among my geraniums. I banged on my windows, but he didn't hear me, too engrossed in his wide-eyed hold on my wall.

But Alf Burrage had heard me, then seen me and then realised what I had been trying to do. There was a burst of gunfire as Alf spotted the cat and vaulted our party fence, firing widely as he came. Several panes in my greenhouse shattered and fell and my plastic waterbutt began piddling in three directions at once. I screamed as I saw him aim one of his pistols toward me, his shot taking out the louver above my head. Mouse finally lost his precarious grip and splattered back down into the alleyway, bolting with his tail between his legs as Alf emptied his barrels after him.

I twice hit a six in my scrabble to phone the police. Blood was not my strong point and it was dribbling on to my hand from where a splinter of toughened glass had pierced my forearm

'Hello? Police?' I just about garbled. 'There's a man in my garden with a gun! Oh my gods, oh my gods, I don't do blood . . .'

When I came to, I could hear the heavy thrum of a police helicopter, high above my house and the wail of out-of-synch sirens in all directions. There was a SWAT team tramping through my vegetable patch, uprooting my brassicas as if searching for a heavily armed gnome. I heard a barked command from the other side of the fence and as one, the team turned and took up a formation around Alf's dilapidated potting shed with the grace of a squad of tooled up ballerinas. I refocused my binoculars so that I had a clear view of the shed door that now had twelve high-powered rifles pointed at it, where in fact one could have pulverized it to dust just by butting it. The group sergeant had a loudhailer to his lips, even though, if Alf was holed up inside he could only have been three feet away from him.

'Put down your weapons and come out with your hands up!' he shouted, above the roar of descending rotor blades, barely containing the onset of his inevitable breakdown.

I strained to hear Alf's reply. Nursing my shrapnel wound, I guiltily hoped that Alf would come out shooting and give the twitchy sergeant a reason to blow him to smithereens. Well, wouldn't you?

A lieutenant was despatched to sneak a furtive peak through the shed's grimy and cracked side window, which he executed with an exaggerated aplomb that by rights should have seen him accepted into RADA, his comic double-take being clearly visible even at this distance.

He scurried back to his commanding officer to whisper his findings which visibly, though disappointedly relaxed the man, who then ordered the team to stand down. As twelve safety catches clicked off as one, I entertained the notion of Alf Burrage swinging by his neck from an old hosepipe inside the shed, but as the nearest officer gingerly opened the door I baulked at the most unlikely of tableauxs to be revealed.

Alf Burrage was on his knees, side on to the door. His bloodied shirtsleeves were rolled up to his elbows and his cap was on the floor beside him, cradling two damp newly born kittens. I could see Mrs Vlastock's Smudge wrapped in his rouched flackjacket on the floor beside them, desperately trying to deliver a third with . . . Alf as her midwife. A rough tourniquet was wrapped around Smudge's back legs and was seeping yet more blood from the pellet wound beneath. Tears streaked Alf's miserable face. Tears. One of the marksmen bent down to help him while Alf stroked Smudge's head and whispered to her. Another of the team appeared with a police-issue first-aid kit and as Alf took the latest arrival to meet its siblings, began worrying at the cat's wound with a pair of elongated tweezers.

The whole surreal scenario appeared to play out in slow motion for me as I watched through misting binoculars. It seems that I had been wrong to dismiss the man as beyond redemption.

After stroking all three kittens one last time, Alf removed his shirt and covered the now sedated Smudge in a move that seemed both utterly natural and at the same time like a forcibly dredged race memory. He apologised through oily tears then offered his wrists in supplication for the sergeant to cuff. The hard-as-nails marksman with first-aider training, having removed the pellet, cleaned and dressed the wound and given her a shot of painkiller, turned and gave a thumbs up as Alf looked over his shoulder just before being helped into the back of the waiting police van.

A month later Alf was charged with cruelty to animals and criminal damage. He wasn't, however, banned from keeping animals, thanks to a petition in his defence from the arresting officers, which was a stroke of luck as it turned out. At his trial Alf announced his intention to open his home as a sanctuary for stray cats while they awaited re-homing. He had apparently seen the light and recognised the error of his ways.

His attitude to people never changed, though. He remained steadfastly the miserable old sod that he had always been. And you really, really wouldn't have wanted to be a pigeon or a seagull or a pizza leaflet delivery boy. He was training those cats up!

6

Making Up the Numbers

He didn't want to die!

He still had things to do. He was yet to make his indelible mark on this world: yet to stake his claim, to carve his name into the damn near immutable substance of the universe that had spawned him.

Okay, so that was probably an overly melodramatic way of putting it, but he was a romantic, a thinker, an ideas man. He had ambition. Lots of ambition. Whatever they said, he knew in his heart that he had been put on this earth for more than just to make up the numbers. He was a dreamer, a grafter, someone who could see outside of the box that he had been born into and effect a change for the good of everyone around him.

It wasn't that he was afraid of dying. He was an atheist. He had no fear of demons wielding fiery pokers or officious-looking angels insisting that he do his harp practice for all eternity. There was no afterlife. You either 'were' or you 'weren't'. What was there to be scared of? And we all had to die eventually, he knew, it wasn't an option. He just didn't want to go yet, that was all.

Positive thoughts, he told himself, think positive thoughts, as he hung out headfirst over the seemingly bottomless chasm, his left foot twisted around the seatbelt of his upturned car which rocked precariously on the ledge onto which it had landed a little way down from the dangerously hairpin mountain pass above.

It wasn't his time to die. He knew that. He still had things to do. He'd think of something. He always did. It wasn't as if this was the first time he'd been in this kind of predicament.

People had always told him that he was accident prone, that he courted disaster wherever he went, and until a few years ago he had been inclined to believe them. He had very few bones in his body that hadn't, at some point in his life, been either fractured or broken completely and one of the exceptions to that great litany of disasters was now taking the full weight of his body as he stared his mortality in the face. He had to admit to having experienced more than his fair share of unfortunate and potentially life-threatening incidents in recent years and, if he hadn't been endowed with such a naturally optimistic outlook, then he would probably have realised sooner that it wasn't just happenstance and that the world *was* actually out to get him.

He had been dragging himself out of an open manhole that he had fallen into when he had first seen the two men, just out of the corner of his eye and no more, really, than indistinct man-shaped shadows. Dazed and confused from his fall, he had thought no more about them until a week later when, having narrowly avoided being flattened by a large falling object, he saw them again, fleetingly, looking out of the window from which the piano had presumably just been pushed. They had appeared clearer this time, though still not enough for him to recall any distinguishing features. He saw them twice more during the run-up to the publication date of his book, each time superseding a seemingly random accident of one kind or another that he had miraculously walked away from with only minor injuries. They were there, just for a second as he had been caught in the backdraft of that exploding shop and again when a tree had landed on top of the taxi that he had just got out of. Each time they had disappeared before he could follow them and find out who they were.

Understandably, he had begun to get a little paranoid,

wondering if perhaps a rival publisher had been about to launch a book on a similar theme to his own and had wanted him silenced before he had the chance to trump their sales. This theory gained gravitas when, a week before publication, his publisher went into liquidation and he found his life's work shelved in the wrong metaphorical sense. For a while after this he didn't see his two would-be assassins, neither was he almost the victim of any inexplicable spontaneous accidents. A coincidence?

A year had passed and he had almost forgotten the mysterious wraiths, so tied up had he been in trying to buy back the rights to his book and resell them to a more solvent alternative, that he had been shocked to suddenly see them again, sitting in the cab of the white van that was about to run him over whilst on his way to sign his new book deal. Having survived this further attempt on his life by the skin of his teeth because of his lightning reactions, he went on to only just survive a further three increasingly unlikely altercations with fast-moving objects, before finding himself trapped between floors in a lift that was creaking ominously from somewhere above him, and it was at this point that he finally cracked, claustrophobia being one of his few anchors to pessimism. After sitting in the corner with his hands over his eyes and screaming for a full five minutes, he heard a cartoon ping and removed his hands to see the two homicidal strangers standing in front of him.

'God, you're a bastard to kill,' said the first, while the second made a quick note on a clipboard. 'You have an unbelievable luck rating for an ordinary!' he continued, turning to his associate who was flipping back through pages with a pencil between his teeth. 'We haven't seen odds like yours since Evel Knievel.'

The spokesman for the pair doffed his bowler hat. 'All respect to you, sir.'

'W-w-who are you and why are you trying to kill me?'

'Oh, sorry,' said the man, 'we're not really here. You're not supposed to notice us. We don't actually exist. We're just a figment of your imagination. You've "created" us to help you to understand what's happening to you. Very clever. We're impressed, aren't we, Nigel?'

Nigel nodded.

'Think of us as the world's accountants. Well, obviously you are already, which is why we look as we do. It's our job to make sure that everything runs to plan, that the numbers add up, so to speak. And mostly it does. Everybody follows the path that's been laid for them.' He paused and leant in a little closer. 'But every now and then someone gets an idea above their station, they try to jump tracks, to . . . better themselves.'

He emphasized these last two words in a stage whisper. 'We can't have that!' he snapped, pulling himself back to his full height. 'It throws the whole system out of balance. You are who you are and then you're not.'

'But that's ridiculous! The whole point of life is to try to make something of yourself, surely!'

The accountant choked and laughed.

'Where on earth did you get that idea? Oh, wait a minute,' he grinned, 'you genuinely think that it's a fair world where "all men are born equal", don't you?' He covered his mouth with his hand in mock shock, 'I am sooo sorry! That's why you keep trying to publish that book, isn't it?'

He turned to Nigel. 'That's why he keeps trying to publish that book!' He turned back to the writer. 'Look,' he said reasonably, 'this is highly irregular, but . . .'

He turned back to Nigel and whispered something to him. Nigel nodded.

'We're prepared to cut you a deal.'

'Go on?'

'You seem like a nice chap, for an ordinary, so we'll stop trying to kill you if you stop trying to be something that you're not. Forget the book. Leave it to whoever's meant to write it. Just be ordinary. It's not as if being ordinary isn't an integral part of the fabric of existence. You all play your part. We don't like killing people, you know, but the status quo has to be preserved.'

There was an awkward silence punctuated only by the creaking of the lift workings.

'Do we have a deal?'

The writer nodded solemnly, but with his fingers crossed behind his back.

There was another comic pop and the lift lurched, stopped and opened its doors. Of his two imaginary friends there was no longer any sign. Shaken by the experience and no longer wholly convinced of his own sanity, the writer settled into a pattern of work, eat, sleep, eat, work for the following five years and during all that time he suffered on average as few as eight random accidents per month, none of which were life-threatening and none seemingly involving mysterious characters with clipboards and bowler hats, until one day whilst driving himself to work, he was suddenly hit by a flash of unbound inspiration. He scrabbled about in the glove compartment to find his notebook and in doing so, failed to negotiate a particularly tight bend in the road. And that is how he came to be hanging by his ankle and facing his imminent demise.

It couldn't end like this. The world needed to know his story. The people had a right to know that their fates were not in their own hands, that there really was no way out of the ghetto. That most of us are only here . . .

just to make up the numbers.

7

Auntie Brenda's Coming to Tea

Dad was a realist, yeah, that's what he used to call himself, anyway. I didn't know what one of those was, back then. I'd thought we were all realists. We were all real, weren't we? What were we if we weren't realists, then: unrealists? That'd make us zombies, or vampires, I'd said. But Dad didn't believe in zombies or vampires. He reckoned there was a rational explanation for every apparently supernatural phenomena that you could think of. He didn't believe in aliens, UFOs, witches or ghosts either, but weirdly he did believe in Jesus.

He doesn't now, though, that was one of the unexpected consequences of Auntie Brenda's visit, but back then he did, back when we were kids, back when things were always explainable with a superior smirk and a 'now, kids, let's look at the facts, shall we?' Let's look at the facts, yeah, Dad, let's look at the facts. It used to irritate the hell out of me, that: the way he always knew the answer, the way everything became another lesson in humourless humility, mental restraint and some longwinded prayer, begging the almighty for spiritual enlightenment. Sometimes kids *like* a little mystery, don't they, sometimes it can be more fun not to know the reality too quickly, to have the chance to run with their imagination just to see where it takes them. But I remember it also made us feel safe having a father who was so unflappable, so upright and sensible, so immutably confident beneath his bristling moustache that aliens could've invaded and he would still have been standing there, thumbing his braces, smug smile rising beneath greying handlebar, explaining to us kids the sheer impossibility of the situation, even whilst they were zapping him with their implausible ray guns and probing his arse with their bony grey fingers, he'd still've been there, I'll wager, steadfast in his indisputable knowledge that they couldn't exist, ergo they *didn't* exist, despite the blinding weight of evidence to the contrary, because, get this, because the Bible had never mentioned them! That was our dad! Infallible to the last. And that's the presiding memory of him that I'll take to my grave.

Confidence breeds confidence, right? Well that's what dad always used to say, and he had a point. If you want to feel more confidant, kids, he'd explained to us, time and again, then first you have to make others feel confident in you. If you look confident and act assertively, then people will start to look to you for answers. They'll believe in you.

All you have to do is to learn to fake it for long enough to glean a real confidence in yourself borne on the wind of other people's adulation. Was that what he'd been doing, I'd wondered afterwards? Was that why so many people had looked up to him? Had he brainwashed everybody around us into believing that he'd known best? He'd always liked people to know his opinions and to dare to disagree with him, which was frequently quite embarrassing, as I recall. I'd had a mate back then . . . George, had been his name. George had thought he was Doctor Who. He'd got this whole reasonably plausible (I'd thought at the time) story mapped out in his head to explain why he'd regenerated into the body of a ten-year-old boy and how he'd hypnotised a childless couple into taking him in and acting like his parents while he completed his top secret mission for the Time Lords. George hadn't been very confident being George, but he'd been ready for anything as the Doctor. My Dad said that was because his Dad was an actor. He had his head in the clouds. He let George read too many comics and watch too much crap on TV. He shouldn't have let him stay up so late or play in the woods on his own. He should've put his foot down when he'd had the chance, Dad'd said (a little too loudly for George's Dad's liking.)

I looked George up recently, googled him, just out of curiosity. He's writing science fiction shows for television now, out in LA. Well respected in his field, apparently. Making a fortune, I shouldn't wonder.

You knew I was going to say that, didn't you? You'd guessed where that story was heading. I'm trying to prove that my old man's methods were damaging to my upbringing, that sitting here in my cell I can now see what it was that made me into the monster I've become! Well, no. I'm neither a monster nor am I in a cell. This isn't really about me. The debate about whether or not nurture can ultimately alter nature will doubtless run till the end of time, but no, that's not what this is about at all. My siblings and I, we came through our childhoods relatively unscathed by our father's ever faithful convictions. We became the people whom I believe we had always been destined to become. My sister's an acrobat in a travelling circus, that surprised no one and my brother, well, he's a drag queen with a residency in a Parisian night club. Again, no great surprise there, except to our father, it would seem.

It may sound like a cliché to say it, but our Dad really was 'harsh, but fair'. He wasn't a cruel man, far from it! He was a disciplinarian, yes, but I'm sure we only got what we deserved.

He always treated us equally, there was absolutely no hint of prejudice or favouritism. He loved us, of that I'm sure, but it had been hard for him, y'know, and an outsider looking in might have misinterpreted our situation, but he was who he was: a man marred by circumstance. Our Mother had died in the process of delivering my sister and he'd had very little help bringing up a new baby and two boys who'd not been five when their Mum had been taken from them. All he'd had, had been his faith: his fervent belief in himself and his zealous belief in his God, so I don't think he did badly, all things considered.

We didn't have much in the way of extended family.

Our maternal grandparents had blamed him for the loss of their daughter and so he had estranged them. You could do that in those days. His own parents had both died young and his elder brother had emigrated to Australia and hadn't been heard from since. They hadn't seen each other for twenty years when out of the blue, we received a letter postmarked 'Perth'. Uncle Bernard was coming home! Dad had tried to appear as noncommittal as possible at this sudden turn of events, shrugged it off with a curt 'we'll believe him when we see him', but I could tell that he was excited. He didn't have many friends on account of his always being with us, so he must've been lonely, even though he tried hard not to show any resentment toward his predicament.

We got out the best china, the set that was usually kept in the display cabinet in the back room, the set that Uncle Bernard and his wife had bought them for their wedding. Uncle Bernard was divorced now, the letter had informed us, but he would be bringing his new 'partner' with him when he came to tea. 'Partner', we were told, was Australian for 'fiancée'. Dad wasn't all that happy with the arrangement, but for once he seemed to have decided to let someone else make a decision for themselves without causing a fuss. He could always do that later, once his guests had settled in.

We were in our Sunday best when their taxi had drawn up outside, each sat in our prescribed places around the dining table, resisting the urge to make paper aeroplanes out of our napkins. It was my little sister who broke rank, cartwheeling to the net curtains as we heard a car door slam twice. Dad had let her, too. I think he was glad of her running commentary as they walked up to our front door, arm in arm, a single suitcase between them.

'She's very pretty,' Sarah had reported back of our newly acquired aunt.

I remember Dad looking quizzical as he greeted his long-lost brother in the hall. It had been strange, I'd imagined, for both of them. The two men had embraced whilst Auntie Brenda had squatted down to greet us kids.

'You've . . . changed,' Dad had said, pulling back to regard his long-lost brother.

'More than you've noticed!' said Auntie Brenda, straightening up and flattening down her skirt. 'That's Digger you're hugging there, Arnie. It's been a while, I know, but really . . . don't you recognise me?'

We'd never seen our dad lost for words before. We'd never seen his stoic mask so much as waiver before, but that was when, just for the briefest flicker, I realised that I'd never seen the real him, the *human* him: Arnold Worthington—the Man, not Arnold Worthington—the Single Father.

For a second there he'd teetered, not sure what to do or what to say, struggling with his suppressed memories. I saw the doubt as it hovered over his features, imagined him flicking through the pages of Leviticus in his mind, searching for an Old Testament verse to back him up for the sermon that was so obviously brewing. And then he changed. The sermon never came. He held out his arms to 'Auntie Brenda' and hugged her tightly for all that he was worth, to the mind-boggling confusion of us kids.

'Kids,' he said, 'say hello . . . to your Auntie Brenda.' And he turned to shake hands with Uncle Digger, smiled and led us all into the dining room, where, in a weirdly factual and unemotional way, our dad explained to us why Uncle Bernard was now Auntie Brenda.

We didn't really understand, nor did we fully comprehend our dad's take on a situation that we instinctively knew there had to have been a biblical law against, nor at that moment did we appreciate that our lives had just changed forever.

Dad served the sandwiches and the cakes, the lemonade and the tea in the way that he always had done: lady adults first, then gentlemen and lastly kids in order of succession, but there was no mention of grace that day. I don't think my siblings noticed, they were too keen to get stuck in with their questions: Sis wanting to know if it was true that everybody walked about upside-down in Australia and my brother going straight for the outed pachyderm in the room.

'So . . . did you get to *keep* it?' he asked, in perfect innocence. He was eight. I looked toward my father, expecting the worse, but he merely choked on a crumb of Victoria sponge and said nothing. At ten, the eldest of our brood, I felt as if I ought to step in and rescue the situation.

'Tommy!' I reprimanded in my best 'Dad' voice, but I must admit, I too was a little curious. 'Why on earth would she want to do that?'

The room had gone silent, all eyes on little Tommy who was busy fiddling with the rabbit's foot key ring that 'Digger' had given him.

'*I* dunno,' he replied nervously, not looking up, probably anticipating the forthcoming clout for his impertinence. 'She could've made a key ring out of it?'

Nobody spoke for a moment and then Dad suddenly broke the ice with a guffaw of Victoria sponge, reacting in a way that we'd never seen him do before. 'What, you mean . . . a "knob fob"?' he queried. 'Ha! Hahahahahahaha . . . !'

His doctor later told Auntie Brenda that he'd had a nervous breakdown, brought on by the stress of all those years of trying to fulfil the role of both parents, coupled by the shock of finding out that his brother was now his sister. But I'm not so sure. It turns out that the sex change was the reason that Uncle Bernard had gone to Australia in the first place. Dad had known about Brenda all along, he just hadn't wanted to admit it to himself. He'd been out of his depth since Mum had died. The character that he had adopted had been a backlash to fears of his own inadequacy. Truth be known, *that* was probably when he'd had the breakdown! This, well, this was more like . . . an enlightenment, an epiphany.

Auntie Brenda stayed with us for a bit after that, just until Dad was well enough to come home. When he did eventually return it was as a different man to the one we'd known.

When I reached eighteen I told him that I'd felt the calling and that I wanted to train for the clergy. He called me a prat and he has never spoken to me since.

8
The Devil
You Know

The kitchen tap drip drip dripped away the seconds of Norman's life, marking time with that same tentative monotony of a hospital heart monitor, missing the beat by just a fraction every now and then, reminding him that nothing in life could ever be perfect and of just how precious his remaining time was. But how had it come to this? Hadn't life once been fun? He felt sure that it had been. He couldn't have got this far into it if it had always been as dull as this: sat here on this hard wooden chair, listening to that dripping tap mixing with the clickety clack of Flo's languorous knitting needles, punctuated as ever by her habitual heavy smoker's wheeze as she completed each new line and began the next. The soundtrack to his life, the rhythms by which he lived. Was this really all there was left?

He used to be interested in things, he remembered, there had been a time when he had been out more often than he had been in. But that was way back before he had married Flo, of course. He had been a dancer, then, not a professional, you understand, it had just been something that he'd liked to do. He hadn't even been that good at it. If he had have been, then he might never even have met his wife. She had been an instructor, and she had taken pity on him, the shy, awkward and partner less one who always left the hall before the couple's dance. She had offered him some private tutelage, he had accepted, and the rest as they say . . .

But the dancing hadn't lasted: the arrival of the kids had seen to that, and so had begun a whole new adventure with their lives awoken to a new dimension of fun.

But even that had had to come to an end eventually. The kids had grown up and moved on to make lives of their own, but he and Flo, they'd been too old and worn out to get back on the dance floor. So they'd festered. Together. In the place that had once been home.

Drip drip, clickety clack, wheeze, cough. 'Shall I make some tea, dear?'

'You didn't finish the last one!' Flo snapped back, as she always snapped when Norman asked her a question, never missing a chance to punish him for accepting those dance lessons all those years ago and thus setting in motion the chain of events that had led them to the here and now. Norman flinched inwardly, suitably chastised, and bit down on his lip. He wanted to argue, to rise to her obvious bait, but what would be the point? She'd win, she always did, because somewhere beneath his once honed alpha male exterior, he knew that she was right.

'Shouldn't you be doing something useful, Norman Dewbury, instead of just sitting there fidgeting and wasting both our lives?'

Norman winced as he instinctively tried to push himself out of his chair, his osteoarthritis making any attempt at sudden movement laboured and painful.

'Oh, for goodness sake,' Flo wheezed, 'don't bother. I'll only end up having to redo whatever you *do* do properly after you've made your usual hamfisted pig's ear of it. You might as well just sit there and wait for Death, like you usually do.'

Drip drip, clack clacketty clack, wheeze, cough, drip. The rhythm of his life, playing itself out, over and over again. Was it worth going on? Flo was still going, whinging and moaning at him like she had been doing since the day that he'd retired. 'And another thing . . . ,' she patronised, but her words were no longer registering, muffled by the dripping that was getting louder and more mechanical, electronic even.

The room was becoming foggy with Flo's cigarette smoke. His throat felt dry and as if he had something stuck in it. His head swam as the bleeping became erratic. Norman screwed his eyes tightly closed and felt his breath catch in his chest. And then suddenly he felt nothing. The dripping tap had become one long, sonorous drawl. A flatline . . .

Norman opened his eyes and realised that he was no longer inside his body. He was looking down on himself from somewhere near the light fitting. Down below, his pyjama clad body lay spread eagled on a hospital bed. A doctor and two nurses were attempting to revive him in much the same way as he had tried to jumpstart his car after its battery had died. Flo was stood a little way away, still admonishing him as had become her unconscious default setting.

Norman became aware of a bright light, burning at his back. The afterlife was calling, offering him sanctuary, a fresh start, away from the pain, the misery and the boredom.

He looked down at Flo and remembered all the good times that they had had and thought about how time and familiarity had allowed those memories to sour. He took a step backwards and felt the light embrace him with its warmth and promise. Drip.

Then he saw it.

Drip.

He almost missed it.

Drip.

Just in the corner of her eye.

Drip.

A lone tear, betraying her frustrated façade.

And it dripped.

It dripped down between her nose and her cheek.

It ran down past her lips where it settled momentarily among the folds and the timeworn wrinkles of her chin.

And then it dripped, and as it hit the sterile white tiles of the hospital floor, Norman's eyes sprung open and he took a deep, involuntary gasp of air into his saggy old lungs.

He heard the blip blipping of the monitor beside his bed, felt the warmth of his wife's hand in his, followed quickly by: 'You stupid old sod, Norman Dewbury!'

Better the devil you know, he thought to himself, better the devil you know.

9
Ahead of
the Game

Yes, doctor, in hindsight, it was a pretty stupid thing to do. Whaddaya want me to say? Excuse me if I'm not always the sharpest tool in the box! The question is, can you get 'em off?

Ouch!

Sorry, yes, I realise that your valuable expertise could be better put to use elsewhere on a Saturday night, but as you're gonna be dining out on my misfortune for weeks to come, I do think you could show a little more sensitivity towards my . . . predicament!

Ouch!!

Please!

If I were to end up with permanent scarring then my career'd be over before it's had a chance to begin!

Chess? Do I play *chess*? Mate, as chat-up lines go that's as likely to win you a fumble as the BNP's chances of winning the migrant worker's vote! What's that got t'do with the price of eggs?

PLEASE!!

There must be something you can put on to dissolve it?

Okay. I'm sorry. But it isn't just painful, it's humiliating! Is there any reason why we can't close the curtains at least?

Thank you. Yes, I tried that. The girl in the shop told me soap and water would do it. It didn't.

Why chess anyway?

And that was when I hit him. Well, I say 'hit' him, *he* said I hit him, but it was more of a slap really. I didn't even draw blood! And, maybe he was right and I don't think things through enough before I do 'em, maybe chess would 'sharpen my wits' and teach me to stay a couple of moves ahead of the game.

But it was the *way* he said it. Stood there all middle-class and white, stethoscope draped round his collar like he thought he was starring in the American version of Casualty, two hands on me tit, talking to me like he'd have to confiscate 'em if I made any further avoidable mistakes!

He said he was going to do me for assault, so I turned on the old waterworks and told 'em he was feeling me up and anyway, I'd specifically asked to see a female doctor and as a female patient that was my constitutional right. That shut 'em up. Didn't help my original problem much, though 'cause they told me I'd either have to wait till one came on shift or come back in the morning.

I've done some pretty stupid things in me time, but I s'pose this just about takes the biscuit. Not the slapping of the doctor, he absolutely had that coming, no, I mean the other thing: the reason why I'm sat here on this cold trolley in nothing more than a tasseled G-string, a pair of red patent thigh-high boots and . . . these.

What's Brian going to say, eh? Brian's me boyfriend, see. He thinks I'm out with the girls from the salon on a Bacardi binge, he'd go nuts if he knew what I've really been doing. Brian's an apprentice footballer.

He misses even more than *I* do. To Brian, everything is a matter of attack and defence. Life's so much simpler for him. He believes that you should find your position then play to it. That's it. That is *all* Brian thinks. But I want more than that. Actually that's prob'ly why I slapped that doctor. He hit a nerve as well as a few nerve endings. I'd love to be able to plan that far ahead, to know exactly where I'm going and how I'm going to get there: checkmate in fourteen moves and all that. Brian says I should stick to what I'm good at, though, play me part for the team, 'leave the hard stuff like thinking to the professionals what are paid to do it'.

I don't know. Maybe he's right. Maybe this is all I'll ever be: a hairdresser in a small town salon with ideas above her station.

Ouch!

No, that other doctor already tried that an hour ago and all it did was give me stretchmarks!

Yes, the one I slapped! Well haven't you got anything stronger? Ouch!

Look, if brute force was going to work, don't you think they'd have come off by now?

No! I don't care if you have got surgeon's hands, that scalpel is not coming anywhere near my assets! Put yourself in my shoes— oh, you can't, can you!

Well she was too sensitive to be a nurse is all I can say if she got upset by that!

The matron came in an hour later with hands like the bride of Frankenstein's and slapped some gloop on me chest that smelled like Swarfega, then stomped back out again in her built-up sensible shoes after telling me to try a gentle twist every few minutes till she came back. She mimed her idea of a 'gentle twist', which looked more like an attempt to get the lid off of a childproof bottle of bleach to me. I suddenly had this mental image of her husband as a short dumpy bloke with a pervert's moustache cowering in a corner wearing nothing but a bridle and a dog lead. Well it's boring sitting here waiting for something to happen! Me mind wanders. That's how I know I'm meant for more, y'see. If I wasn't, then I'd just be content with what I've got like my mum always was. They all think I'm thick just because I was born on an estate and I left school at fifteen. Alright, I don't know much, but that's just 'cause I've never had the chance to learn much, right? I'm not stupid. I've got a brain like everybody else. I've just never had the opportunity to use it properly.

I've tried. I've tried reading stuff that I know nothing about. We've got a little library in the staff room at the salon, it's all books that clients have left behind when they've been having a treatment. The only ones that ever get thumbed are the Black

Lace ones, which seems like such a shame. All that knowledge just sitting there between the coffee percolator and the wax strips and no one else in there has even read so much as the cover blurb. So I pulled out this one with the weird title. I think it was by that bloke who used to be the waiter in Fawlty Towers. Summit about 'the bloke who thought his wife was a hat'. Weird. It was all stuff about people with strange brain illnesses. Way over my head, but I s'pose you have to work up to books like that. You can't just go in cold and expect to understand the secrets of the universe in one go, can you? That'd be like a rocket scientist trying her hand at a back, sack an' crack. Don't bear thinkin' about!

Tracy said I was being daft. Tracy's my boss. She said that people's brain capacities are finite, that you can't just make yourself brainier by reading clever books. If you're born thick, she said, then you'll always be thick. It's like with animals, she said. You can teach a dog how to bark for his dinner, but you can't teach him to say please and thank you. I don't like being called a dog any more than I like being patronised by pompous twelve-year-old doctors, but as she's my boss an' all, I didn't feel I could slap 'er. Which is why I spiked her spritzer with speed at Tara's hen-do instead.

A brain's like a big sponge, innit?

That's how I see it, anyway. It's floating around in yer 'ead, soaking up all the things you see and all the things you read. Sometimes, when you get older, if you've had a really full life, your brain sort of overloads and you start forgetting bits. I've seen that with some of my Ladies. They call it 'dimentions' or summat. I s'pose the trick is not to take in too much in the first place, but I've got a long way to go before I have to worry about that!

So, Dr Smug, I'll have you know I *have* been thinking ahead. I decided to go to night school to try and learn a bit more about stuff, to show people that I ain't as thick as I look.

OUCH!

Shittin' OUCH!

Oh, God, thank you, thank you, thank you!

I take back everything I said about your shoes! Ouch. Will these marks go down, d'you think? I mean, I'm grateful and all, but they do look a bit angry.

Savlon, right.

Double-sided tape. Yes, well it was my first time! I needed to make sure they'd stay on while I was upside down.

I *did* think it through! This was all part of my big plan! I needed to raise some cash so I could go back to college. I'm not stupid, y'know! Shaking yer booty's s'posed to be easy money, right'? It's a means to an end. It's Fleur's little hairdresser brain trying to go one step ahead of the game. But in hindsight I s'pose supergluing me tits to tassels wasn't a very forward thinking thing to do.

10

Christmas within the Catchment Area of an Ofsted Recommended Junior School

Sebastian and Griselda locked eyes across the frost-hardened lawn as he poured a kettleful of boiling water into her bowl, splintering the thin layer of ice that had developed over night and sending a plume of rapidly dissipating steam into the freezing atmosphere. And in that instant, as they waited for the water to mix and cool for her, an understanding passed between them, something primal, elemental, and Sebastian knew then that there was no way that he could do what he had been sent out there to do.

He looked over at her sister Letitia, munching obliviously on the stewed lentils, barley and pak choi with which he had been fattening them up for the past three weeks. Phenola had let Samson choose which one was going to be for Christmas and which for New Year. She'd thought it might toughen him up a bit if they were to teach him where his food really came from and she'd been concerned at just how easily he seemed to have accepted his wayward uncle's effete life choices when he had 'dropped by' the previous weekend, so she wanted to make sure that his weirdy hippy tendencies wouldn't rub off on her son. But Sebastian couldn't do it, not in a million years. He may not have shared his brother in law's vegetarian leanings, but a cold-blooded killer he was not. If she had been that worried that keeping a pet might make Samson go all nancy like her brother, then she should've insisted that the little shit do the slaughtering as well, but oh, no, couldn't let him get his precious hands dirty, could we, there weren't enough aloe vera-infused wetwipes in suburbia for a mess like that.

'Oh, for pity sake, man up, Sebastian!' shouted Phenola from the sunken patio behind him. 'It's only a bloody chicken! You're supposed to be his role model, the great hunter-gatherer!' she paused briefly while she fished around in her handbag for the keys to her four wheel drive BMW. 'Now,' she continued, having found them among the various lotions, potions and electronic accessories that constitute the contents of the young professional woman's everyday luggage, 'I want to see that thing plucked, washed, stuffed and basted by the time I get back with mother and her . . . "man friend", is that clear?'

Sebastian didn't reply, nor did he turn to face his aspirationally obsessed wife.

'I want it in the oven, Sebastian. And don't get feathers everywhere. Rosella only cleaned that floor yesterday!'

He heard the car door slam and the spattering spray of pea shingle against the slatted fence as she roared out of the drive and he turned just in time to see her pull onto the road without so much as a passing glance for pedestrians or other road users.

He turned back to his flock and they looked back up at him—
'the one who brings the food', a blend of hope and blind faith in
their innocent ovid eyes. They had no reason to fear him. They
had never had a reason to fear anyone in their short lives in the
eggloo. He knew that if he reached out to either one of them they
would simply squat down and lift their wings in supplication for
him to stroke.

He hadn't realised quite how close to the birds he had allowed
himself to become these past months, but they were just such
beautiful, peaceful creatures and he had come to prefer it out here
with them, even on a frosty Christmas morning.

'Daaaaaaad!' rang out from within their new-build-detached-
four-bedroom-house at the smart end of suburbia. 'It's broken.'

'Already?'

What was he thinking 'already'? Of course 'already'! He'd had
the fuckin' thing for almost ten minutes, of course he'd broken it.

Sebastian turned and trudged back across the crispy white
garden to meet his son at the back door.

'It's rubbish!' Samson proclaimed, offering up the remote-
controlled helicopter that they had bought him. Well, half of it
anyway. The rest of it lay in a wide arc of destruction, along with
several more mangled-beyond-repair toys that he had languidly
unwrapped less than an hour ago. Sebastian surveyed the scene of
plastic and cardboard carnage. Little shit, he thought to himself,
but his 'parent' voice, lodged somewhere at the back of his
conscious mind like a bound and gagged demon with nails
through his feet, attempted to heap blame on the toy
manufacturers who had deliberately failed to take into account
that the children most likely to fall for their cynically targeted
advertising campaign were unlikely to understand the terms
'gently', 'carefully' or 'don't jump up and down on it if it doesn't
obey you as instantly as your stupid fuckin' parents do'.

His rational mind won out, though. Samson's attention had
drifted from his broken toys and he was now glued to the
television screen, absorbing adverts for yet more plastic crap

whilst attempting to fit an entire selection box of chocolates into his fat little face without chewing.

'I want that, Dad,' he gurgled through the chocolate, pointing toward a freeze-frame of the toy's price, now only half what it had cost the day before.

'We bought you one,' Sebastian said, scanning the roomful of debris for any remnant of it.

'Broke,' replied his son, holding up an arm that should have been attached to a robot's body. 'Are we going to stab the chicken, now?' Samson continued, hauling his squat little body toward the remains of his presents and extracting a plastic pirate's sword from the teetering stack.

Sebastian looked at his watch. Phenola wouldn't be back for another half an hour. He wondered idly about the chances of Mister Puri's mini-mart being open today and if it was, whether he would have had any non-frozen chicken pieces in the chiller (Phenola considered turkey to be the common man's choice).

A plastic bullet hit him squarely between the eyes. He recoiled in reflex and cracked the back of his head against the dining room door.

'We can get her with this!' came a shout from somewhere out of his dazed view.

His head bleeding and his vision foggy he took a faltering step to steady himself and slipped on a half slobbered on bar of chocolate, which duly ground its way into the pile of the Axminster like a caramel and peanut dog turd as he surfed toward an imminent, painful and ultimately expensive cranial appointment with a wide screen, high definition television set.

Things were a little clearer when he woke up. His son was standing above him poking his eyes with his sword.

'DAAAAAD! WAKE UP! We've got to kill Griselda! Can I pull her wings off, dad, can I?'

When Sebastian had been Samson's age he had still believed in Father Christmas: the big snowy-bearded philanthropist who, if you'd been a good boy during the months prior to the big day, would bring you a present to reward your behaviour. Ah, the 'Good Old Days', a simpler time, a time when people got what they deserved at Christmas. It wasn't his son's fault that he believed that he had a basic human right to everything he wanted as and when he wanted it, it was society's.

Neither was it his fault that he had no appreciation for the value of what was given him, that particular failing was his and Phenola's. Well, mostly Phenola's, to be fair. He would have been happy to have lived within their means, to have stayed where they were, but no, that'd been selfish, apparently. Samson deserved the best, Samson had a right to the best and they had an obligation to do all that was in their power to give it to him.

But what about the chickens? Did they not also deserve the best life that he could give them? They didn't ask for much and in return they were happy to donate an egg each per day to the cause. What had the kid ever done for him?

Phenola, her mother and her mother's man friend returned to find Griselda and Letitia pecking at a pair of fairtrade mince pies with cream from a Royal Dalton bowl on the kitchen floor. Sebastian was in the process of draping prime bacon rashers across the dismembered corpse of her butter-basted son.

'I know what you're thinking,' said Sebastian, looking up from his work sheepishly. 'These were supposed to be for breakfast tomorrow, but I knew you'd only want the best for our little Samson.'

11

The Fourfold Truth

It depends how you look at it, really and no two people see their world in exactly the same way, do they? A tree is a tree, some might say, it's got a trunk, some branches, a presumed but unseen root system beneath it and a load of leaves in the summer. And that would be a reasonable assessment to somebody who may just be passing one by on their way to something of greater interest to themselves. But what if that person were an arborist, a specialist in trees? To them that description wouldn't be nearly enough to cover what they could see before them. They could tell you its genus, in Latin probably too, they'd know its average lifespan, whether it was likely to bear fruit or nuts, whether it was deciduous or evergreen. They'd even be able to describe the exact shape of those leaves and the precise shade of green to use if you wanted to paint an accurate representation. Then show that same tree to an artist and ask them to tell you what they see . . . and you get the picture, I'm sure.

Four separate witnesses on four opposing corners of the same junction see four unique versions of the same accident. Which one's telling the truth?

Jamie Findle, 38. A landscape gardener. Knew the victim. She'd been a dinner lady at his school back when. He hadn't liked her. She'd shouted at him once when he had tried to jump the queue, she had humiliated him in front of his friends. They'd had a name for her back then, 'Grotbags', because she looked like a character in a kid's teatime television programme. Jamie thought about that when he was staring at her lifeless body in the road. She'd got old, he'd thought, her long curly black hair had turned grey. She wasn't as fat as she had been when he'd known her, either. But she still looked like a witch. Maybe even more so with all those wrinkles and hairy moles.

It had all been a bit of a blur for Jamie. He'd just stepped out of the paper shop, having had a tussle over correct change with Mr Puri, the newsagent, and had been about to cross the road when he had heard the furious dinging of a bicycle bell and had had to jump back onto the pavement as Old Grotbag had whizzed past him on her rusty old bike, bellowing at him in that same patronising voice that she had used on him when he had been thirteen. He had felt that same pang of humiliation and had been about to respond with a witch-themed insult when he had seen the black cab that his nemesis had not. She hadn't stood a chance. Maybe if she hadn't have been going so fast, perhaps if she had not just turned her head to berate him . . . who'd ever know for sure? It had definitely been her fault, though, according to Jamie Findle.

Tracy Fenton, 35. Hairdresser. Miss Featherstone had been a client of Tracy's in a semi-regular capacity for as long as Tracy had been working. She had inherited her from her mother when the latter had retired and although her ministrations were only rarely required, Tracy had always regarded

Miss Featherstone as one of her favourites. Unlike a lot of her clients, Miss Featherstone had never been one to use her time in Tracy's adjustable chair as a form of cheap psychotherapy. She had never been a moaner nor a whinger, in fact, she had rarely given away anything more personal than her observations on the day's weather and her recommendations or otherwise on previously visited holiday destinations. What Miss Featherstone had been, however, was her prime source of local gossip. Miss

Featherstone had been the doctor's receptionist. Very little of the town's business passed her by. Tracy cared deeply about her ladies, perhaps too deeply for a professional, she'd often wondered. The background information that Miss Featherstone had been able to supply her with had meant that she was often in a more knowledgeable position to be able to deal with her client's various 'issues', to comfort them, to gain their trust and their confidence. An essential ingredient in her trade.

Tracy had been late opening up that morning. If she hadn't have stopped to pick up the post and allowed herself to get waylayed by that letter from the council, then she wouldn't have been waiting at the pelican crossing as Barry Ogilvy, that creepy bloke who always winked at her when he saw her, had run the lights and driven both Miss Featherstone and her bicycle into the tarmac. He'd caught her eye for a split second as he'd gone past and it'd given her goose bumps. In Tracy's opinion, it had been deliberate.

Angus Spode, 22, Student of Life. He hadn't known either of the protagonists. He'd been an entirely impartial bystander. He'd been waiting for a bus on the corner of O'Malley Street at the time. Probably not the best angle for a witness to this particular incident as his view was obscured slightly by the arrival of a double-decker bus.

He wouldn't have needed to catch that bus, though, if it hadn't have been for a cyclist. They were lethal, man! He'd been the designated driver, that night, so he'd only had a couple, and they hadn't even been large ones. He'd had a couple or three tokes off Cindy's spliff too, but that'd been before they'd gone out so he hadn't been worried about that, even so, he'd taken precautions, he'd gone the back route home just in case some rookie copper who hadn't filled his quota sheet for the evening had pulled him for that dicky front light.

And anyway, one light's gotta be better than none at all, right? Which was exactly how few lights the cyclist who had pulled out on him had had on! That lucky sod had got away, but Angus hadn't been so fortunate. He'd skidded in the wet, hit the bank and rolled the car into a ditch.

It'd taken him ages to get out of his seatbelt, what with being upside down an' all, and even longer to get the unconscious Cindy out of hers and onto the verge. He'd been a bit shaken, but surprisingly unhurt, Cindy, on the other hand, had been a bit of a mess, but breathing steadily so he'd known she'd be alright. The car had been totalled. He briefly pitied the poor sod who had owned it, whoever that was. He'd laid Cindy in his best approximation of the recovery position and used her phone to call for an ambulance—he was a bastard but he wasn't scum. She'd understand when she came round. The last thing she'd want was to see him go down, he told himself as he legged it across the fields.

He'd been on his way to visit her in the hospital when he'd seen the accident. Ordinarily he would've avoided police questioning like the plague, but he'd convinced himself that this was for Cindy. It might not've been the same cyclist, but they were all alike, they all thought that the rules of the road didn't apply to them.

He'd told them what he'd seen.

He'd seen the old lady and he'd seen the taxi, though he couldn't recall any traffic lights. She'd come across him from the left, so technically she should've been the one to give way. He didn't remember hearing a horn so the driver couldn't have seen her till the last possible moment. It was a terrible tragedy, but in his opinion, cyclists should stick to cycle paths and stay off the roads. They don't even pay insurance or road tax!

Hamble Fortescue, 68. school governor, local area chairperson for the Women's Institute, Conservative Party member and co-ordinator for the Garfield Road Neighbourhood Watch Association. Hamble had first met Angel Featherstone when they had been partnered as volunteers to chaperone their local candidate on her door-to-doors. Angel had remarked that they had resembled ladies in waiting, with their matching sprayed blue carnation buttonholes and the potential MP's insistence that they never stray closer to her than five slingback feet. Angel had been a distinct upper-middle to Hamble's lower-upper and so it had been a surprise to them both that they had hit it off quite so instantly and become such firm friends thereafter. Angel had been an absolute brick when Charles had died so suddenly on the eighteenth hole, she quite honestly didn't know what she would have done without that book of prescription slips that Angel had managed to procure for her from the surgery. And she could not begin to express her gratitude for the way that her friend would quite happily bump patients that had been waiting weeks for an appointment with Doctor Sorbet just so that she could squeeze her or one of her friends from the WI in at the last minute. Of course, it hadn't all been one-way. She was thinking now of that distressing accusation of pilfering that had been made against poor Angel last week. Outrageous. In a country full of scoundrels and scroungers who between them manage to hoodwink 250 million pounds out of the public purse each year in dodgy benefit claims, they choose to go after a sweet old dear who wouldn't hurt a fly, and a Christian, no less, merely for forgetting to pay for her shopping! Not stealing the Crown Jewels, mark you, no, just a couple of bottles of gin and a lemon. Well what would be the point of being the widow of an ex-mayor if one couldn't rest a little influence now and then?

Hamble Fortescue had been watching out of her drawing room window from her townhouse on the corner of Garfield Road, waiting for her friend to arrive. She had been late. Crimplehorne: her solicitor, had been there for almost an hour and had snuffled his way through an entire plate of macaroons already. And his time didn't come cheaply. He was claiming not only to be able to win her case for her, but to instigate a counter claim against her accusers for defamation of character. And then she had seen her, rounding the corner on that trusty old bicycle of hers, peddling as fast as those varicosed calves would allow. Hamble had dropped her Wedgewood teacup at the precise moment of impact, scattering bone china fragments and Darjeeling in a nuclear blast zone patterning all across her Stoddard rug. It all happened so quickly too. One minute Angel was steaming toward her like a runaway train, the wind whipping up her frizzy grey locks so that she looked for all the world as if she were being harangued by her own personal storm cloud, the next she had joined the ranks of squirrels and hedgehogs as carrion paté for a magpie's sandwich. It was her nerves talking, she knew that. It was the sight of her best friend squished in the road like a spinster pancake that had made her start thinking along such inappropriate lines. Just another few feet and she could have been stuffing her face with whatever macaroon crumbs hadn't yet made it into her solicitor's belly, just a few more feet and she could have been on her way to exoneration rather than exaltation in the hereafter.

And he hadn't even stopped, had he? He had knocked the poor dear from her mount and then driven over her with all four wheels. And if she hadn't been mistaken, he had been laughing with his fare as he had carried on past her window.

Common little man too, had the bearing of a criminal. And he had never once shown the slightest interest in Neighbourhood Watch. That said it all!

The truth from each one of them, but who should I believe? There is a tree that stands on the corner of Garfield Road, an Oak. It was clearly visible to each of the witnesses as well as both of the protagonists, though curiously none of them mentioned it in their statements. When I asked them to describe it to me during their interviews they were each able to paint a relatively accurate depiction, although again, nobody seemed to notice or have any strong opinion regarding the cyclist's eye-line level bough, upon which, incidentally, Miss Featherstone's decapitated head was later found. There are flowers at the base of that oak tree now. They could be daffodils, they could be lilies, I really couldn't say.

12

One Man and His Dog

Best part of the day, this: the evening constitutional. Just me and him. No matter what the day brings, we always head out together at the same time for a circuit of the village and the chance to pick over our day's thoughts, to ruminate, if you will, on the 'what ifs' and the 'why didn'ts': our way of clearing out the cobwebs ready to start tomorrow afresh whilst walking off our dinners before turning in for the night. Well I say 'our' thoughts, but Christ knows what *really* goes on in his mind as we amble round the block, probably nothing more than 'wayhay, like the smell of that!' as we pass Fifi and 'her from a few doors down' on the other side of the road.

I don't know, I'm guessing: I've no idea what's going through his mind at the best of times! Eat, scratch, fart, sleep, eat some more, would probably not be that wide of the mark, but who can say? They might be more intelligent than we credit them, I might be doing him a great disservice. Just because *I* can't make head nor tale of his desperate attempts to communicate, doesn't mean that others of his species don't comprehend him perfectly well! I could be living with a genius and I wouldn't even know it.

I don't think I am, though and it doesn't bother me either way: I wouldn't love him any the less for being the dumb animal that he appears.

Me and him.

Me and him against the world is how it's always been and that's just fine by me. No matter what we've been through, I can honestly say I've never seen his loyalty waiver for so much as a millisecond.

Since the very first day we met there's been an uncanny kinship there, a special bond. Language difficulties aside, I've always felt that we had some kind of empathic connection between us, as if we shared something deeper than the rest of the family did with either of us, something primal and ancient that transcended the specieal divide.

A sort of telepathic link. Oh, God, I hope it isn't that! I really wouldn't want him to know what I'm thinking right now. Or ever, come to that! Maybe I'm anthropomorphosizing here, he probably wouldn't care what I wanted to do to Sarah, hell, he'd probably even want to join in and help me to do it!

So we walk. We follow the same route that we follow every evening. He likes that. I think it helps him to relax. At the weekends we usually go over the park, but the park's always full of people and I think people make him nervous, which feeds back to me too and then I get all agitated myself. I much prefer our evening strolls, same as I much prefer 'her from a few doors down' to 'her indoors' and I know *he* does. It's written all over his face every time he sees her.

I've often used these walks to fantasize about what I'd do to her, Sarah, that is. She's always been jealous of our relationship and she takes it out on him something wicked.

I've killed before, you know, when I was a nipper. I had quite the vicious streak in me back then. Birds, rabbits, you name it, I killed it. What? Well we all do that stuff when we're young, don't we? We don't know any better. Besides, I'm a meat eater, a carnivore. If I couldn't bring myself to kill it then I shouldn't be eating it. Not that I want to *eat* Sarah, good God, no! Bony little bitch.

I would like to kill her, though and I'm sure he would too. Hold on. Another lamp post. Here we go again.

Yeah, killing Sarah . . .

Ah, here she comes, right on cue. Her from a few doors down, doing exactly the same route as us at exactly the same time, but in reverse so that we pass 'incidentally' at the furthest point from our respective homes, just by the bus stop. Anyone watching would think we'd planned it, but no, not unless we've got a telepathic link with them too. The lead goes taut. Someone's trying to muster some testosterone!

A smile? Is that all we can manage? Again.

Right, that fixes it. I *am* going to kill Sarah. As soon as we get home. I'm going to gut her and skin her like I used to do those rabbits and then bury the bits at the bottom of the garden. And the baby. I suppose I'll have to kill her as well. Or should I leave that to him? We could pretend someone had broken in whilst we were out walking, that they'd taken advantage of our daily routine to catch her at her most vulnerable moment. The first thing we'd known about it was when we'd got back from our walk. We'd tried to stem the bleeding which is why our dabs are all over her. Her a few doors down would take pity and want to comfort him and I might even get a sympathy shag out of Fifi.

Yeah, that's what I'll do. As soon as we get home that bitch is mine!

13

The Visionary

'He says he isn't really the Prime Minister. Apparently, he swapped clothes for the day with an urchin who just happened to look like him.'

'Oh, well, tell 'im he's free to go, then.'

'Really?'

'No, Smiler, of course not really! Do I look stupid? He's a politician, lying's in 'is blood. Go back an' tell 'im why we're 'ere.'

'Ain'tcha got no ambition?'

'Ambition,' he says, like that's all y'need in life t'get y't'the top. Ambition.

The Prime Minister visited our school once, back when 'e was on the campaign trail.

'E did this great speech for the six o'clock news about how the 'future belonged to us'. All we lacked, apparently was vision and ambition. Up till then all I'd ever wanted t'be was a Time Lord, but I s'pose I knew deep down that that wasn't 'appenin'. But 'e got me thinkin'. What I really wanted t'be, though was an astronaut. Yeah. Maybe if I worked really hard . . .

An' then 'e went away and reality kicked back in. Ha! Ambition's all well an' good if you 'ave the means t'achieve y'dreams. It was a comprehensive, for Christ's sake. 'Ow was I ever going to get on an NVQ astronautin' course coming from my background, eh?

'You might wanna scale it down a bit,' the careers officer said, 'work up to it. Like, maybe you could be the bloke who helps him into his suit, y'know, checks 'is seals an' 'is pipes an' shit.' Yeah, right, like that's bound t'be 'ow it works, innit. Y'start at the bottom an' work up. Equal opportunities for all. We're born as blank slates an' it all comes down to how ambitious we are as t'where we end up. Don' make me laugh!

Ambition. Yeah, tha's my problem. I'm jus' lazy. I give up too easily. I should'a studied harder at that comprehensive. I could'a got a GCSE in astro-bloody-physics, could'a got meself on NASA's youf trainin' programme. I could'a bin runnin' ground control by now!

'Ello? Estate Boy calling, ya' got any jobs goin' for a kid with a GCSE in media studies (the most qualified kid in my year, I might add) an' a good working knowledge of how t'stay alive after dark in this part'a town?

No? What, not even tea boy or apprentice pipe attacher? I don't mind startin' at the bottom and– oh, they hung up.

But that's the problem, y'see. The middle classes always like t'think that all this country's problems can be blamed on the fact that the lower classes are too 'appy t'wallow in self pity while *their* taxes pay to keep 'em in a luxury lifestyle. Why would we want t'better ourselves whilst we're bein' paid t'do nothin' all day? No ambition, no branded aspirations.

We all come inta this 'ere oyster naked, penniless an' equal, right? Earth t'Prime Minister! Look around you, talk to people, and not just t'people you know, either! It's easy just t'look down from your ivory tower and tell us we're not aiming high enough. Talk to us. We're not that diff'rent to you, really.

We're all human beings, we're all hardwired by the media t'want th' same things out'a life. We see 'the ideal', same as you do: all those adverts for exotic holidays and expensive consumer goodies, only for us they're just that little bit harder to reach. See, when you start lower, you've got further t'climb.

You don't put as much work or money inta teachin' us the basics as you do the middle classes. Why? 'Cause you've started t'believe your own hype, that's why. You think it's wasted on us 'cause we got no ambition.

So, Mista Prime Minister, we're 'ere t'prove you wrong. You told the people (and by 'people' I mean the ones what believe what they read in the press, the ones who you've got convinced that the biggest threat to national security is their own shadows), you told those people that last year's riots were 'disaffected youf who'd rather steal than work'. You blamed it on anarchists, yobs, you said, who were just jealous of what you 'ad and whose only motive was wanton destruction and violence for the sake of violence. No shut up, you've said your bit, it's my turn t'speak now!

They were wrong to do what they did out there: the lootin' an' th'fightin', the smashin an' th'burnin'. An' nobody wants t'see that 'appenin' again. But see, th'more you disempower them, the more you blame them for livin' in the conditions you heap upon them, the more you make us suffer for your own greed, ignorance an' indifference toward those whom you see as 'less worthy', the more likely you are to spark it all off again!

Now, we don't want t'see that.

We might be scum t'someone of your breedin', but may I remind you: I've got a GCSE in media studies, I can read an' write. I'm your worst nightmare, mate: I'm not just scum, I'm scum with ambition!

I tried writing to my MP, that is still the proper way t'do things within a democracy, I believe, but d'you know, my letters just kept on gettin' lost in the post. I tried t'get in t'see her, but her surgery seemed t'be booked up even further in advance than my doctor's! So I wrote to you. You are, after all, my personal representative on the world stage with, correct me if I'm wrong here: a constitutional obligation to have one of your minions at least acknowledge my letter? But . . . nothing. Saw my address and decided I was statistically unlikely to vote for you, did you?

Anyway. That's why I'm here, why *we're* here. I've come to speak t'you in person. Cut out th'middle man.

Let me introduce you to my team.

Smiler here, you already know, he's the one who said he could clean your windows a pound cheaper for cash than your usual windowcleaner. It was Smiler who accidentally left the window unlocked in your back bedroom and his ladder up against the wall. This is Mark, Smiler's probation officer, who's here to verify that Smiler is working legally and paying his taxes and has a very poor memory due to his dyslexia.

Mr Crimplehorne here is my 'no win no fee' solicitor. He's here in an observational capacity to make sure that I don't break any laws and that you don't tell any fibs about me breaking any laws, i.e. we have not just 'broken an' entered', as your friend here put it. Smiler here was invited in and the rest of us came in through a conveniently open window. Technically we're squatters, with squatter's rights. By the way, you do realise that according to your law, you are obliged to make sure that no avoidable accidents befall us whilst we're on the premises? Good. The fella' holdin' your plod down is Pete. Pete's a judo black belt. He was also once a plastic p'liceman so he knows the legal definitions of reasonable force and self-defence. He's actually doing you a favour making sure your plod doesn't do us the harm he's promising to. And this is Mister Puri. He's my boss. He's here to verify my references.

So. Now we're all acquainted I'll get to my point. I'm not 'appy, Mista Prime Minister, not 'appy at all. I feel that your system 'as let me down. But I also feel that that same system is letting you down too. What you need, mate is an apprentice, someone who can advise you on how t'deal with the ordinaries, t'help you to avoid another face-off with the dispossessed. I could learn on the job an' I'm happy t'start at the bottom an' work up, y'know: make the tea and check y'seals an' shit. I've got ambition, y'see, and vision. You taught me that. One day I'm gunna make it all the way t'the top. So whaddaya say, eh?

14

Independence Day

'Premiership footballer in drunken nightclub brawl!'

'Cabinet minister in five-in-a-bed kinky gay sex orgy!'

'Suburban newsagent, 50, has affair with retired hairdresser!'

'How shocking!'

'How decadent!'

'How dare they?'

Outraged of Hackney asks: 'Don't these people appreciate the obligation that they have to those who put them where they are today?'

Incensed of Aylesbury writes: 'By accepting this podium status, they are effectively entering into a contract whereby they have a duty to display nothing short of the purities of sainthood and to appear the very paragons of public virtue.'

'String 'Em Up!' decrees an editorial in The Daily Rumour.

That, says the common consensus, is the price of fame.

But is it, though, is that a fair expectation? And are there no escape clauses for those who neither courted nor hankered for it in the first place?

Raggi Puri didn't like being famous, but it came with the job. He hadn't actually wanted the job, truth be known, but, as was the story of his life, he hadn't had the balls to say so at the time and so that had been the hand that he'd had to play. That was Raggi:

the man who'd stuck when he should have twisted, the startled rabbit in the world's shiny headlights. Everybody knew Raggi, and his business, by its very nature, was everybody else's business.

But if he had wanted notoriety then he would've stayed with the band (who incidentally had signed their first major record deal the day after he'd left them), or he would've kept up his running and gone on to represent his country as his coach had anticipated. But Raggi had never had such dreams of riches and grandeur, he'd never been an ambitious man. Perhaps because he had always known that his fate had been predestined from birth.

Raggi's parents had moved to Britain in 1948 in the wake of India's independence—the Fall of the Raj—with the hope of building a better life for themselves and their future brood. Mister Puri Senior had worked hard in a factory making cars by day and by night had waited tables in his brother's restaurant in order that he could put enough aside to fund his great ambition. They had scrimped and saved for more than a decade until in 1961, he had become the proud proprietor of one of the first Asian corner shops to open in the suburbs of London. Raggi and his sisters had been born in the rooms above that shop, they had known nothing else, only hazy stories of their Indian ancestry and their father's struggle for his own personal independence from a culture of class division and religious conformity. It would have broken Mrs Puri's heart if the business that had both provided for them all and had eventually killed her husband had not continued in the family name after his death. It was Raggi's destiny, she had insisted, should he have dared to have believed otherwise.

Mr Puri Senior was mourned by the community that his little empire had sired. Raggi, his only male heir, had been forty at the time and, having worked with his ailing father since leaving university, was the only real choice to inherit the shop. His father had fought a long and bitter war of attrition against one greedy local supermarket, whose ability to keep its prices artificially and illegally low had been backed up by the local shares-owning MP and the superior buying power of its parent company. It had been a war that had ultimately taken its mortal toll on his fluctuating blood pressure.

Asian corner shops had been a dying breed by that time, Raggi knew. Due in part to the choking corporate noose forever tightening around their collective necks, yanked by the market dominance of these impersonal supermarket chains, no longer content with their huge out-of-town city-state monstrosities, but now sweeping through the suburbs in their vainglorious quest to wipe out independence once and for all, like bubonic plague rats massing in a shit-strewn sewer, but equally to the reluctance of a generation of well educated, high-flying sons and daughters of forties immigrants to work day and night for peanuts in the waning family trade.

But Raggi had been resigned to his fate. Truth be told, he was a lazy bugger at heart. Oh, he'd worked the hours alright, but he'd never really done anything that hadn't been laid on a plate before him.

At twenty-five he had accepted an arranged and loveless marriage to his mother's third cousin's daughter, Sham. Raggi wasn't a traditionalist. Having been educated in multicultural twenty-first century England, he didn't even think of himself in Hindu terms, and it wasn't as if he had been coerced into it, either. He had just felt that it was what his mother had expected of him and had submitted quietly and without a fight. In fact, his father had secretly hoped that his son might have rebelled at the suggestion, shown a little of the great Puri backbone that had brought them this far, proved to him that he had been right to make him his successor instead of his brother-in-law, Talin. But Raggi, as usual, had plumped for the safe option, the route of least resistance. He hadn't wanted to stand out, to draw attention to himself, so he'd just gone along with what he had thought other people had wanted of him and played the cards that he had been dealt.

He had an image and a reputation to uphold, he'd told himself, his father's image and his father's reputation. He'd been a respected member of society, a pillar of the local community. His counsel had often been consulted on matters of local importance by the press as a so-called 'community leader'. Raggi had an obligation to his father's customers to uphold the values that had kept this family solvent for so long.

Raggi had been the owner of 'Puri's Papers' for a decade before he had noticed Angie Fenton (The Daily Rumour and Men At Work Monthly). He had known her for years, of course, everybody knew Angie. She owned the hairdresser's on the other side of the street, which she used to manage until she'd retired and passed it on to her daughter, Tracy. He hadn't been able to put his finger on quite what it had been about Angie that had been so different that day: the spark that had ignited the passion that he hadn't even been aware that he was capable of harbouring, the switch that had been flicked that would illuminate the light that would go on to brighten his life in ways that he had never even imagined possible. Was it that firm and curvaceous body of hers, the body of a woman half her age? Was it the brightness of her inner light or was it what she represented to him: independence of mind, body and spirit? She had smiled at him as she had collected her paper, that same smile that she had always smiled. She had collected her change, given her customary 'seeya!' and exited his shop as she had done every morning for more years than he cared to recall. Had he imagined that extra sparkle in her eyes that day, that coquettishness that had flashed so briefly, but enticingly above her drooping designer glasses? He'd told himself that he had, as he'd fought down that juvenile flush of hormones as she had stepped back out into the day. He had suddenly become aware of just how long twenty-four hours could be and had admonished himself for allowing his tired old mind to wander like that. He was a married man! Sham was only a room away preparing their meal for later, and their boys wouldn't be far away either, probably plugged into a machine of some sort, conditioning their malleable teenaged minds for some apocalyptic future war or other, and his mother, the great matriarch of the family, who among her many omnipresent attributes Raggi was sure included the ability to read minds. It had been at this moment that that harlot from the estate had come in to ask him to put yet another of her thinly disguised 'massage services' cards in his window. It was in retrospect that he put his disproportionate outburst down to guilty stirrings on his own part!

He had made a special effort the following day to look as good as a balding and spreading, middle-aged man could look without causing alarm bells to clang for his wife. Angie had arrived at 09:41. She'd smiled, paid for her paper and had waited for her change. He had wanted to say something, anything to delay the inevitable, but he hadn't been able to think of a single thing! He was out of his comfort zone and into the realms of possibility, which was a place as foreign to him as the country of his parent's birth. She'd winked at him. It'd been a definite wink. A smile and a wink and then she was gone for another day.

The following morning Raggi had woken even earlier than usual. He had thought of nothing else all night, but of watching Angie Fenton removing that outrageously skimpy summer dress in a darkened corner of his shop, down the back somewhere, amongst the cornflakes and the toilet rolls, whispering his name as she stripped. But 'seeya!' was all that she had ever said to him and so it had been Sham's voice that he had heard.

He resolved that day to engage Angie in conversation. When she had not arrived by midday, Raggi had begun to worry. She hadn't cancelled her order so she must have been ill. By 4 o'clock he was suffering from a mixture of mild panic and middle aged tart withdrawal.

At 17:15 salvation had come in the form of a telephone order from old Mrs Batts (The Daily Rumour and Tattoo Fetishist Quarterly) at the far end of the street, only a few doors further along from Angie Fenton. He hurriedly gathered her requirements together into a plastic carrier bag and shouted up to the flat to Raggi Junior who was hastily pressed into service behind the till, his brain still connected to the ether by two almost permanent earplugs.

He'd had no inkling as to what he might say to her when he got there. He would have liked to have had more time to prepare, but an opportunity as perfect as this might never arise again and besides, he knew that given the time, all he really would have done with it would've been to talk himself out of it. And he wasn't doing anything wrong, was he? He was merely making a couple of deliveries, technically Raggi Junior's job, but hey, he could do with the exercise!

As Raggi left the shop he almost collided with Harold Goodman (Zion Times and Brides Monthly), who had been on his way in for a packet of cigarettes. Raggi Junior not being quite eighteen yet, his father slipped down his first snake, returning himself to square one and missing a turn. It was at this point that Mrs Puri Senior chose to make her entrance, hobbling through the beaded curtain from the pantry like a Force-spent Yoda, as if summoned by Raggi's doubt-laden conscience to remind him of who he really was.

'Why not send the boy, Raggi?' she advised as she passed Mr Goodman his purchase and took his proffered note. Had she really read his mind? Was she taunting her son into admitting his intended deception? 'Your place is behind the counter,' she reminded him, passing Mr Goodman his change and dismissing the ever so slightly effete florist with a moralistic scowl, an oblivious Raggi Junior beside her, bobbing his head in time to a rhythm that only he was party to. 'Your father would never have left his post during a shift, you know.'

He faltered momentarily, Jiminy Cricket clinging to his sagging shoulder and expressing his agreement by nodding his tentacled head dolefully.

But something spurred him forward, a defiance that he had hitherto never mustered, convincing him to risk ignoring one of his mother's 'edicts-disguised-as-a-reasonable- suggestion'.

'I need the air,' he ad-libbed uncharacteristically, stepping back onto the pavement before the elderly widow had the chance to offer a maternal fresh air-themed counterargument.

Had Angie somehow bewitched him? He certainly felt intoxicated, wired, as if none of his life up until that moment had really mattered to him.

He made it all of two doors down before being flagged by Fleur (Hair & Beauty, 'anything gossip-ridden'), on her way home from the salon, to ask him if he had her copy of this month's Celebrities In Compromising Positions in yet. He did. So he directed her back towards Raggi Junior—whom he knew, however zombified, would have moved heaven and earth to find a magazine order for young Fleur (randy little bastard that he was)—thus extricating himself from what could've proved a lengthy and mind-numbing round-up of the day's backwash gossip, and thus sidestepping snake number two and landing him on a metaphorical ladder up the road. Head down to avoid further interruptions, he ploughed on with his journey. As he passed the gate of No. 24, the wizened old face of Florence Dewbury (Knitter's World and Medical Mysteries Monthly) suddenly popped up from behind her privet hedge.

'Good evening, Mister Puri,' she said as he pulled up sharply, almost losing Mrs Batts' semolina pudding from the top of his bag, 'nice night for a stroll?' She winked at him knowingly.

'D-d-delivery,' he stammered guiltily, feeling as he had felt that day way back in his teens when his mother had caught him teaching his younger sister how to smoke. He ducked pathologically at the sudden memory, flashed an embarrassed smile and kept walking, hoping that she would sense his need for urgency and not try to regale him with stories of her frail old husband's adventures on the geriatric ward.

'Young Raggi revising, is he?'

'I believe so, Mrs Dewbury, yes. If you'll excuse me?'

She nodded and tapped the side of her nose.

It was turning into a nightmare!

Only eight more houses to pass and already half the town knew that he had left his post! Doubts began to fester in his mind. What was he thinking? There was no way that a man as public as he could possibly conduct any kind of illicit dalliance without it becoming public knowledge before he even got home! He was being stupid, entertaining such outrageous ideas just to escape the mundane monotony of his existence.

Who did he think he was, for goodness sake? And where on earth had he suddenly got the idea from that he was capable of independent thought?

He delivered Mrs Batts' groceries without incident nor conversation and turned back towards Angie's house.

What was he doing? What did he intend to say?

He felt a rush of adrenaline coursing his veins, a feeling that he hadn't felt since his university days: limbering up for a race or stepping up to the microphone. He straightened up, slicked his wispy fringe back with a sweaty finger and . . .

As his hand touched Angie's gate, a second hand fell simultaneously on top of it.

'Ooh, sorry, Raggi!' said Tracy, Angie's daughter (True Crime Stories). 'Were you delivering? That's very sweet of you. I'm going in, I'll save you the trouble. Mum's got a dose of flu, wouldn't want you catching it. That'd be awful, wouldn't it?' she rambled. 'If you got ill, then we'd all get ill!'

'Thank you,' was all that he could muster as he handed over the paper and turned tail.

'I'll tell her you called!' Tracy shouted after him, but he was already two houses down the next snake. 'She'll be dead chuffed,' he caught on the breeze.

He stopped outside No. 34, Harvey Rial, the painter's house (Artist's Muse and The Daily Scandal). He could feel his heart pounding, bursting to break free from the tomb that had been his chest.

'You alright, mate?' enquired a voice that he didn't recognise: somebody whom he didn't know, what we in the trade would call a 'passer-by'. Raggi leant forward and steadied himself against Mr Rial's wall, seeing the occupant's curtain twitch once in response.

'Sir?' continued the transient, offering a supporting arm. 'Do you need to sit down, can I call somebody for you?'

Raggi took a deep breath and stood up. He smiled at the person who didn't know him.

'Thank you, but no,' he said, pulling himself up to his full height, a height that he had never before quite realised. 'My heart is not about to give out, my friend, quite the opposite. It is only now waking up.'

'Oh . . . if you're sure.'

It should have been a deflated Raggi Puri that headed back along the road to his shop. He had, after all, failed in his attempt to woo Angie Fenton by delivering her paper by hand, but he was actually feeling quite pleased with himself on this warm spring evening.

'Evening, Mr Vartes (Practical Alchemy and Build-Your-Own-Ark-In-50-Easy-To-Assemble-Collectable-Parts)!' he said as he passed the local nutter carrying a Puri's Papers-stamped bag of comestibles.

'Mrs Stevens (The Worrier's Almanac and Amateur Detective)! Nice night for a stroll, eh?'

Mrs Stevens smiled politely as she snuffled past, weighted down on the one side by another of his bags.

He had taken a big step today, even if he hadn't actually shown the dog the rabbit, as it were. He had done something spontaneous, something devil-may-care and it had made him feel alive for the first time in as long as he could remember and possibly ever.

'Good to see you, Ms Fortescue (Class Warfare)! I trust you are well?' he enquired of the busybody from the big house on the corner.

The adrenaline was still there, still pumping through his heart. He had forgotten what that had felt like, how much more awake it was possible to be.

It was a long time since he had felt this positive, this cocksure and fancyfree.

'How are you, Dr Sorbet (The Lancet and Voluptuous Vixens)? Ha! I bet nobody ever thinks to ask you that, do they?'

Raggi stepped back into the shop, whipped away the surreptitious copy of Big Jugs Monthly that Raggi junior had been drooling over under the counter and yanked out his earphones. He cuffed him playfully around the head with the magazine and said: 'There is more to life than tits, Raggi. Go back to your revision. Go and learn to *be* someone.'

He replaced the magazine on the top shelf and surveyed his kingdom. His kingdom. Not his father's nor his mother's, but *his* kingdom.

It had been an important day for him. He hadn't needed to talk to Angie Fenton. All that he had needed had been to admit that he *wanted* to speak to her, to have taken control of his own destiny and to have set off *to* speak to her. At fifty years old Raggi Puri had finally come of age.

The first thing that he did the next morning was to order a new sign for the shop which would read 'RAGGI'S INDEPENDENT STORE'. The second thing he did was to slip a note inside Angie's newspaper.

15

The Last Laugh

There's a lot to be said for dying on the toilet.

Alright, on the face of it, it may not seem to be the most dignified of ways to go, but at least it's a private affair, you wouldn't have to try to put a brave face on that final agonising death rattle, you won't be expected to come up with a supposedly spontaneous, witty final line and you are in the perfect position for that embarrassing post mortem moment when your muscles relax and your corpse begins to divest itself of any excess bodily waste that may still have been lingering in your tubes. So much kinder on the poor sod who finds you, don't you think? Top tip, though: if you're alone in the house, never lock the bathroom door. Just in case.

And you're in auspicious company too. Elvis died on the loo. As did Judy Garland and King George the Second. It's more common than most people might think. But it is something of an obvious design flaw in your basic human being, if you ask me. An essential daily function that can put the heart under such an intense amount of strain, raise your blood pressure and in extreme cases result in instant death?

. . . as Leonora was just discovering for herself.

One minute she'd been settling down with her favourite prayer book for a pre-service ablution and the next, a violent coronary spasm had mugged her of the life with which God had entrusted her, twenty minutes before the first parishioner had been due to arrive for the early.

Sixty-five isn't old, these days, not for the English upper-middle, anyway, she should've been good for at least another twenty, but that's the thing with life, you just never know when it's going to come to an abrupt and undignified end in the vestry cubicle, straddling the porcelain with your knickers around your ankles.

The first that Leonora had known about it was when she had suddenly found herself standing in the arrivals hall of what she had taken to be a large and bustling international airport. Her rational mind had tried to compensate for the disconcerting continuity lapse. She was dreaming, yes, had to be, she'd nodded off on the bog again.

That would explain why she was now wearing the dress she'd been wearing the night she'd first met Donald, way back in '65— the floral one with the starched petticoat that had cost her the equivalent of a month's wages from the biscuit factory, and not the autumnal tweed church warden twin set that she'd set out in that morning.

But she knew dreams, she'd spent decades suppressing them, denying the nature that Satan continued to taunt her with on a thrice-nightly basis. This wasn't a dream, it was too real, in fact it was even realler than the reality she had just left behind. But if this was real, how come she had pert breasts again after all these years and where had the wrinkles, the baggy eyes and her infamous collection-collector's perma-scowl all gone?

Leonora wasn't stupid. She'd quickly put two and two together and accepted that she must have been dead.

She allowed herself a rare smile. She'd been right, then: if she was here, then God *did* exist and there *was* a heaven, not that she'd ever doubted it herself, but so many of those around her had mocked her for her faith over the years (including Donald) that she decided to savour the last laugh for a second.

Although she hadn't necessarily wanted to die just yet, Leonora felt a huge wave of relief wash through her restored teenage body. It felt as if she had been holding her breath for six and a half decades and could finally now exhale and be free. Life had been okay, she supposed, but she'd always seen it as a proving ground for the right to earn a better, eternal life up here in heaven with Him. And she had obviously passed that test because here she was. She'd have liked to have been able to see Donald's face right now. She'd married him because he'd seemed like a good man. He hadn't been a believer, but she'd felt sure at the time that she could have won him round to her way of thinking. It wasn't as if he'd been a Satanist or a Muslim or anything. In fact, they'd had much the same core values when they'd met, he just claimed not to believe that the world had been created by an omniscient being as a test for the mortal sinner's everlasting soul. Donald had died at fifty-nine whilst being 'administered to' by three prostitutes, none older than his granddaughter, in an Amsterdam brothel. Oh, the shame of it! He had gone off the rails somewhat in later life, had something of a midlife crisis. Said he'd been put on this earth to have fun and so fun was what he was going to have.

'Go Grandad!' had been the general family consensus. Well, they wouldn't be laughing now!

'Name?' snapped the angel, although he looked more like a jobsworth immigration officer than one of the Almighty's heavenly host.

'Leonora Spatchcock,' she replied haughtily.

The angel tutted rudely and flicked his eyebrows heavenwards.

'*Real* name.' he snapped impertinently.

'That *is* my real name,' she answered indignantly.

The angel spoke quietly into a small microphone clipped to his collar.

'Oh,' she hurriedly added, 'do you mean my maiden name? Trent.'

'No, madam, I mean the name that you booked under. What . . . hold on.' He turned away to speak to his collar again. Then he turned back to her and suddenly smiled, adding: 'Where do you think you are, madam?'

Leonora returned the smile unwittingly. 'Heaven, of course.'

Two more angels suddenly appeared, each taking one of her arms and steering her toward a door marked 'HELP' to the side of the concourse.

'Next?' said the officious angel as she was led away.

Inside the featureless, white side room was a short row of plastic chairs and an unmarked door. One of her guides showed her to a vacant seat while the other passed her a ticket with a number on it. She got the distinct impression that they were sniggering to themselves as they left.

She was not alone in the waiting room. She was surprised to find herself sat beside what she took to be a woman in a head-to-toe black burqa. The woman's eyes looked as shocked as she imagined her own to look at that moment. Next to her covered friend sat a man in the full traditional get-up and flowing grey beard of an Orthodox Jew and beside him, an orange-robed Hare Krishna, his brass cymbals closed neatly on his lap. Nobody spoke nor so much as acknowledged their neighbours, each presumably as worried as Leonora was, that they had somehow arrived in the wrong afterlife.

She had waited patiently for what had felt like an eternity as each of her unlikely companion's numbers had been called in turn. Each had entered the unmarked door and none had returned.

'Number six thousand six hundred and sixty-six, please!' she heard from the room beyond. She stood, opened the door and stepped inside.

'Take a seat,' said the angel who seemed to be dressed as a doctor, gesturing without looking up toward a psychiatrist-style couch. She sat uneasily on its edge while he finished making some notes.

'So,' he said, sliding his spectacles closer to his eyes. Leonora idly wondered why an angel would need glasses. 'Does the name "Skooter Breeze" mean anything to you?'

She considered his question then shook her head.

'Should it?'

'Oh, dear. Even worse than the last one.' He took off his spectacles and sipped from his mug of coffee. 'Where do you think you are, m'dear?' he asked, rather patronisingly she felt.

'Heaven,' she replied firmly. Perhaps this was a part of the test?

'You caught religion, then, did you? Well,' he said, standing up and replacing his spectacles on his nose, 'you look genuine, but I'll have to do a full examination before I can refer you for compensation. We get an awful lot of fakers through here, y'know. They think they can hoodwink us by claiming to be Mormons or Scientologists, but we know a believer when we see one.'

'I'm sorry, I don't follow you, doctor. I'm a church warden and a Sunday School teacher. Have I displeased Him in some way?'

'Very good!' the angel/doctor confirmed. 'Well, I say good, I mean good from the point of view of a partial refund, but bad in a "Hedonistic Holidays: Do What Thou Wilt Shall Be The Whole Of The Law" kind of way. Tell me,' he said, peering into her pupils with a magnifying lens, 'did you have *any* fun down there at all or was it all just abstinence and birch twigs?'

Leonoro, shaken by his Aleister Crowley reference and unsure just how much this test was intended to push her, steadied herself, kept her face as stoic and unruffled as she could and said: 'I followed the Lord's scriptures to the letter. My only crime was to inflict my beliefs on the heathens and the unrepentant sinners of our parish—' (a thought had suddenly struck her) '—and . . .' (surely He couldn't hold this against her) 'and . . . to insist that Donald had a proper funeral despite his . . . evil ways.'

The psychiatrist stepped back sharply as she spat her words with more vehemence than she had expected.

'I see . . . ,' he eventually said. 'Well, Ms Breeze. I'm sorry to say, but you do seem to have caught a severe case of religion, down there. On behalf of the company, I can only apologise, stamp your claim form and wish you a speedy recovery.'

He gave her a sheaf of paperwork and bade her a good day, showing her through to baggage reclaim where she was met by a familiar face.

'Donald?'

'Eh? No, Beezer Floom, luv. Have we . . . ?' the baggage handler put down her stored effects and removed his hat. 'Oh, my unsubstantiated deity! It's you! Leonora, wasn't it? We met on holiday, didn't we, down on Earth? Ha! You caught the bug, didn't you. Did you get over it? Ah, no, you've still got it, haven't you? You poor thing. We had some fun, though, didn't we, at the start, I mean. Before you got all . . . ,' he smiled. 'Tell me you at least went out with a bang?'

Leonora/Skooter said nothing, tears welling in her eyes.

Beezer/Donald passed her her bags, smiled kindly and replaced his cap. 'If you fancy a shag, some time, for old time's sake . . . you know where to find me.'

16

Returns

Wait a minute, isn't that . . . ? No, it can't be. It's just my mind playing tricks on me. Thirty years on and I'm still seeing his face! It certainly looks like him. Can't be, though, on the returns counter, In white and pastel pink-striped dungarees, looking like a post-op Andy Pandy? Mark Stark, the hardest bastard in our school? In a pink cap with tinsel round the rim and a flashing name badge that reads 'Hi, I'm Mark, how can I help you?'

Bit of a coincidence if it isn't, then. But what'd he be doing here, now? It was a long time ago, but that nose is unmistakeable. Mark Stark. My worst nightmare . . .

—'Oi, Spud!'

(He called me Spud 'cause my name's Howard. No, I could never work that one out either.)

—'Oi! You deaf or summat?'

'What?'

—'Have I kicked you yet today?'

'You spat on me this morning and you stuck chewing gum in my hair—'

WHAM! Walked straight into that one. Right in the knackers again. The swelling's barely gone down since he did that yesterday.

—'Oi!'

I'm reeling on the ground, fighting to get my breath back. He kicks me again, base of the spine this time.

'Thank you,' I croak, tears welling.

—'Thank you, Mark!'

'Thank you . . . Mark,' I blub.

Mark's Dad's in the Army.

He reckons this is how it is in the Army. Discipline and respect, he says. His Dad told him that it's the Army's job to keep the scum in line, to make sure we understand the chain of command, to weed out the weaklings and the subversives, to cut out the cancer that is individuality. Last term we were taught that if we wore our trousers as tight as the current trend dictated, then our testicles would shrivel and we wouldn't be able to make babies when we needed to. Mark's Dad said that was a good thing. Fashion stops the weak from breeding. Mark has decided to help matters along with his own little eugenics programme, by givng all the weeds a daily nut-kicking. Mark's going to join the Army when we leave school. Then he'll be allowed to kill scum like me, or so he tells me.

I got out the first chance I saw. I moved down to London to live with my Mum's sister. More chance of work in the city, I'd said. I've been back once a year since then, for Christmas dinner. In an' out. Didn't stop to look around. I'm only back now 'cause my Dad just died and so I've taken some time off to be with my Mum. I've been tarting the old place up a bit for her, mending things my dad never got round to and painting over his nicotine stains. I'd bought a pot too many, so I was taking it back for a refund, but this has stopped me in my tracks. Mark Stark. I never expected to see that nose again. I'd've expected him to have been working with an entirely different sort of hardware by now.

I was nervous about coming back here, I have to say. The village holds nothing but bad memories for me. I've put all that behind me now, rebuilt my life. I've lived away for twice as long as I ever lived here. I told myself that nobody would recognise me, hell, nobody would even remember me, everyone from those days would've grown up and moved on. And then I saw Mark and, despite the fact that he's lost his hair, he's wearing glasses and he's packing a walrus worth of blubber beneath that effete all-in-one, I still feel like that twelve-year-old who had his fingers broken in a vice during woodwork class.

I can't move. What if he recognises me, what if he hasn't changed, what if . . . ?

I can't do it. What would I say? How would he react to the fact that I'm still alive, that I've done okay, that I've . . . got kids, older than we were when we last met?

It's just a pot of paint. It isn't worth the risk.

I spend the night mulling it over, back in my old bed for the first time in all these years. Have I really changed? I thought I had, but have I? 'Hi, I'm Mark, how can I help you?' I'm the customer, not the victim, he's the assistant, not a mindless army-brat thug. Doesn't that confer even a modicum of power to my court now? What was the worst he could've done to me? Offered me a credit note instead of my money back? What a ridiculous situation! I'm forty-six years old, *we're* forty-six years old! We're different people now, aren't we?

I sleep and I dream about the past . . .

'Oi, Spud! Can you smell burnin'? Y'blazer's on fire! Hur, hur, y'get it? Yer blazer's blazin'!'

I still have the scars on my back. Lost most of my hair. Got a detention for leaving the classroom without permission. Got another one from the headmaster for snitching on Mark for doing it and had to pay for a new uniform out of my pocket money. Had to apologise to Mark in front of his parents for threatening to 'get him back' and got a broken nose from Mark for refusing to thank him. I wake up in a cold sweat.

I decide to go back to the shop and confront him, well, not confront him as such, more pass him my tin of magnolia and ask, no, *demand* my refund. Face my demons. Show him that what he did to me at school hasn't in any way affected the rest of my life. I'll even pretend not to have recognised him. That's got to wind him up!

He's not there when I get there, though, there's a girl on

returns instead. I'm not sure, but I think I recognise her too. Wasn't she Mandy Monroe? Christ, what a state! She used to be gorgeous at fifteen. No, it can't be. They can't all still be here! She was a right cow, that one, convinced the whole school fancied her, and to be fair, most of them did, even a couple of the teachers, if I remember correctly!

It's funny, not that I dwell on these things a lot, good God, no, but whenever I have thought of these people, I've always presumed that they'd gone on to achieve what they'd set out to back when. Mandy was going to be a model, yeah, who could forget that! Too good to breathe the same air as me. What the hell happened?

I step up to the counter and heft my paint pot into view.

''As it bin opened?' she asks, as I clock her name-badge.

'No.' I reply, deliberately not catching her eye. Mandy had been way out of my league. I would never have let myself get caught looking at the likes of her. Mark would've killed me! And even though I wouldn't shag her now if my life depended on it, I still can't break the habit.

Mandy drags the pot toward her, scans it and enters the code it supplies her into her till.

'Receipt?' she asks without looking up. I comply, she stamps it and hands me my refund.

''Ave a nice day,' she says, then sits back down and retrieves her magazine.

The whole process had taken less than two minutes. I walk away, slightly miffed not to have been recognised and now desperate to know what had happened to her.

As I leave the shop, my mind elsewhere as I walk, I bump straight into Father Christmas standing in the gap between the two sets of doors. A pile of Christmas special offer leaflets scatter to the four corners to fall like soil in the aftermath of an explosion as Santa flattens a cardboard sleigh packed with empty gift-wrapped cardboard boxes. An artificial tree goes down with him, its various glass bells and baubles shattering like pixie grenades against the floor all around him. Instinctively I reach a hand down to help him up, but he's floundering like an upended turtle fighting with a plastic tree.

'Mark, you fat twat!' scolds Mandy from somewhere over my left shoulder. Santa's beard has slipped and his glasses have got entangled with the tinsel. That's when I notice something that I'd previously missed. So typical of me, that! I've allowed myself to become so utterly absorbed in my own 'stuff' that I have completely missed the obvious: the dynamic between these two old foes of mine.

'You can't afford to screw this up!' the sexiest girl in our year continues, pushing past me to try to pull the hardest bastard in the school out of the demolished display that he's trapped in. 'I told ya, ya lose anuvva job an' tha's it! You're out fer good this time!'

As she bends forward, the gusset of her overtaxed dungarees gives way in a perfect line along the crack of her flabby arse. There was a time when I'd've given good money to see such a sight, but not today, not now, I've moved on.

The manager has called for a forklift to get Mark up from the floor. The more he flails, the more he destroys. It's a pitiful sight. I could have spat on him, I could have kicked him hard between the legs, but, as the headmaster had told us often enough: 'It's one thing to kick a man in order to *put* him down, that's nature, and to be encouraged: the strong will always rule the weak. It fosters defiance and ambition in the weak, inspiring them to be stronger and to fight back.

'But to kick a man when he's *already* down, to exact revenge on an already defeated opponent? That is a sign of weakness and cruelty: that is telling your enemy that he was right all along.'

I can't help it. My suppressed titter becomes a giggle, then a full-on guffaw as the forklift truck arrives. Mandy gives me a look of pure hatred, but says nothing in the presence of her betters.

I take a last look at him as I walk back to my life, the man who taught me how to be me and I say: 'Thank you, Mark.'

I don't know if he got the punchline.

17

A Study in Claustrophobia

Seven billion people. Seven *billion*! That's how many human beings are currently sharing the fifty-seven billion, five hundred and ten thousand square miles of floor space that the earth has to offer. Put like that it didn't seem as tight a squeeze as he'd first thought it was. By Harry's rough calculation that gave every man, woman and child alive something like eight square miles each to play with. So why had they all decided to come to the same doctor's surgery on the same day and at exactly the same time? Obviously they hadn't really, as he would find out later when he tried to get a table in the cafe over the road.

At least a third of the world's population were already in the queue ahead of him and the remaining third? Well, they were blocking the pavements and the roads and every other bloody shop he tried to get served in between these two ports of call, sniffing, stinking and plotting away wherever he needed to be.

Eight square miles. They had eight square miles each. So why did they have to do everything together and all at the same bloody time? Of course, the mathematics weren't really that simple. Eight square miles each was about what you got if you divided up the earth's land space equally between everybody on the planet. What it doesn't take into account, though, is the arid deserts, the inhospitable jungles, the mountain peaks and the arctic wastes where only the most ardent of the people-phobic attempt to survive.

Harry didn't know how much space that would leave everyone else, but he felt sure that it'd be more than the majority of people seemed to think they needed.

He wasn't all that keen on people, was Harry, he never really had been. As far as was politely possible he had always tried to keep out of their way. He much preferred the company of flowers to the company of his fellow homo sapiens. 'You know where you stand with flora and fauna,' he had always said, to the one person that he had had to commune with on a daily basis—his boss, Mr Batts, who had owned the florist on the corner of St Kitts Street where they had both worked together for the past three decades. 'Flowers don't judge you. Flowers don't lie to you. Flowers don't care what you look like or what unfortunate personal defects that you may have been born with.'

Harry had never married. He had never even had what could be described as a 'significant other'. Harry's life had been devoted to the study and the arrangement of his beloved flowers. He had created his own little world in which he had been perfectly content. Until now.

He was feeling a little hemmed in today, somewhat claustrophobic, as he sat there in the doctor's waiting room waiting to see the doctor and, as had always been the way when he found himself in the enforced presence of people, he had begun to sweat. And not just a trickle, either, it could never be just a trickle, could it, but a full-on steaming salt water torrent. He mopped at his fallow pate, but rather than soaking up the pooling puddle, his soggy handkerchief merely smeared the flood closer to where his fringe had once sprouted, causing an instant tide to cascade from his forehead down onto his cheeks and nose, there to flow unchecked onto his already drenched polyester-mix shirt. He squelched from his seat to the surgery when his name was called, like a beflippered frogman wading from the surf.

'Ah, Mr Goodman. Come in, take a seat, do,' said his doctor.

'Now. How's it been going? The last time I saw you, you were . . . let me see,' he thumbed through his patient's records, 'retiring! That was it. So,' he continued, removing his spectacles and squinting across at Harry, 'how has that helped with your problem?'

The doctor clasped his hands together on the desktop between them and affected a well honed, but ultimately less than convincing expression of care and humility for his fellow man.

Harry dabbed at his slippery forehead with the doctor's proffered tissue.

'I'm afraid it's getting worse, doctor,' he said. 'Look at me! Every time I see another person I start leaking like an Australian anarchist.'

The doctor peered in closer like a tortoise studying a lettuce leaf. 'Hmm,' he hmmed, noncommittally, handing him another tissue, 'you do seem rather damp.'

'Damp?' Harry parroted, 'I'm soaked through! I've had over-active sweat glands since I was a teenager, but this . . .'

He pulled at his sopping shirt for emphasis and it slapped back against his chest with a shlopp.

'Hmmm,' the doctor hmmed again. 'Well, sudden retirement can bring on some quite odd and unexpected psychological side effects, Mr Goodman.' He passed him a towel. 'Perhaps it's time for a new hobby?'

'It's not a hobby I need,' Harry countered, dripping exasperation. 'Can't you give me something to stop the flow? Isn't there some kind of anti-anti-water retention drug out there?'

The doctor laughed. 'Mr Goodman,' he schmoozed, 'I can't give you any more medication. Your problem, although manifesting itself in a very real and uncomfortable way, is entirely psychosomatic. You have to learn to overcome your fear. They're just people like you and I. Nobody is out to get you. They're not stalking you, Harold, they're just sharing the same space. Granted,' he acquiesced with a halting hand, 'there are too many of the blighters, but there's nothing that you or I can do about that, so we have to just learn to deal with it.'

Outside the surgery, Harry lit himself a cigarette and drank in the nicotine hit with the ferocity of a vacuum cleaner fitted with a stair-runner nozzle sucking up a grate full of ash. He decided against a coffee in the sardine tin of a cafe opposite and headed for home, taking the long way round in an attempt to avoid the massed masses that were waiting for him on the main roads.

He was at his wits' end. There had to be something he could do? The doctor had said that he should get himself a hobby. Was it too late to retrain as a chemist and develop a virus that would wipe out all mankind? And did wanton genocide count as a hobby anyway? He'd certainly never seen a glossy mag on the subject in Mr Puri's paper shop.

He couldn't shake the feeling that he was being followed, even though every time he checked behind himself there was nobody there. It had been like this ever since Mr Batts' grisly murder at the hands of the Vigilante Crimper, one of two local serial killers who had recently been apprehended in the immediate vicinity. The other, the Pedestrian Killer, had lived only two doors away from him! And people wondered why he was paranoid? Maybe it was something in the air around here? Or the water? What if the authorities had mixed a little too much of their patent Anti-Anarchy solution in with the fluoride that they put in the supply and it had had the opposite effect? Instead of pacifying the population it was turning them into murderers!

He poured himself a whiskey and sat down at his kitchen table. The wind had dried him off as he had walked, but now he itched all over.

Perhaps the doctor was right. Maybe it was just a reaction to his changed circumstances, that and the unusually high local mortality rate. He had always hated being around people, that was unlikely to change, but he had to get past this irrational fear that they all wanted to kill him. Nobody even knew him! He had spent the bulk of his life sitting on his own in the back room of a florist's. He had kept his head down. He had stayed out of everybody's way. He didn't have any friends, but at least he didn't have any enemies, so why was he so convinced that somebody wanted to kill him? Stupid.

It was one of those irrational fears like people had of spiders or snakes or the dark, even. He was sixty-five and in reasonable shape for his time of life. There was no reason to think that he wouldn't live another twenty years at least. He finished his drink and, feeling a little calmer, changed into his working clothes, collected his secateurs and went out into the garden to tend his roses.

He had been merrily pruning for a while when he felt a salty rivulet run from the well on the top of his bald head, down between his eyebrows, along his bulbous nose and drip down onto his exposed wrist. He looked around the garden, but could see no sign of an intruder. Stupid. Irrational fear. Nobody wants to kill you, Harold, he reminded himself.

He continued with his deadheading, but just couldn't shake the nagging feeling that he was been stalked around the beds. Beads of sweat begat streams that flooded their banks and returned him to his previous near amphibious state. He tried repeating the names of the various flowers and plants in order to clear his mind and when he ran out of those he moved onto bugs and diseases. He dragged his lawnmower from the shed and plugged it into the insulated socket on the garage wall. As he pulled the starting lever he noticed a stray wire beneath the handle, but before he could react, he just had time to see a lone droplet of sweat fall from his chin and land right on top of the bare wire.

Harry didn't die instantly.

He lay there amongst his roses for almost a full minute whilst nobody came to his rescue. Nobody saw him die. And nobody was seen to slink away into the night clutching a pair of wirecutters, giggling maniacally behind their hand.

Harold Goodman died alone doing what he liked best. It's how he would've wanted it.

18

The Nation's Favourite

Geoffrey really didn't know, well, he couldn't be sure. He certainly wasn't certain, he was clear about that, so he'd rather not be drawn on the matter, if that was okay with everybody else?

Any matter, that was. He knew he ought to have had an opinion, opinions were important, they were after all the bedrock upon which an individual's personality was founded, but he didn't like to make a fuss. He was happy just to go with the majority flow, like you were meant to, as the rules of a happy society dictated. He didn't like the idea of standing up to be counted, he didn't have enough to say, so he'd always just taken the soft option. So what did that make him, then? Mr 'Find Me A Fence And I'll Straddle It'?

He was set-dressing, background colour. He was the dullest man on the planet.

Was there a God? Don't ask Geoffrey, he didn't know. He'd been raised to believe so and yes, if asked his take on religion on any kind of official documentation he would have felt inclined to have put 'C of E', like most white non-Catholics that had been born and raised in England would have done. He didn't feel Muslim nor Hindu and he definitely wasn't Jewish—he'd have noticed that—but he never went to church, except for family hatch, match and despatches and he never prayed, not even in emergencies. But he did wear a St Christopher for luck. Did that make him a believer? He really couldn't say. He was hedging his bets, he'd decided to wait and see, agnostic to the last, that was Geoffrey.

He knew that he was heterosexual, but he also knew that didn't count as it wasn't exactly a conscious decision, so to use that example as evidence of an underlying forthrightness was something of a sticky argument. He preferred tea to coffee, but that was no more a choice than was his sexuality—his tastebuds decreed coffee too bitter.

And what did it matter anyway? He lived in a world where people were obsessed by choice, yet failed to notice that their options were becoming more limited every day. 'The bigger the shop: the greater the choice!' they would argue. Oh, really? The greater the choice of things that have been chosen for you to choose from by a corporation with a vested interest in influencing and thereby limiting your choices!

But there are so few small shops, these days! Your 'pro-choice' big shops have seen to that: further limiting your choices, but under the rather ironic banner of 'freedom of choice'. And take politics. Three separate parties, each one styling itself as a legitimate individual option, but each one made up of people from identical social and educational backgrounds, each one peddling the same message in the same accent, but each one trying to convince you that their take on that choice is best and that you actually do have . . . a choice.

Geoffrey knew all of this, he wasn't stupid. He had *chosen* not to make a choice because he *knew* that he didn't have one.

The Nation's Favourite Poetry: it was a book that his aunt had given him last Christmas. He had been carrying it around with him ever since, dipping into it whenever he found himself with five minutes to kill. It was an anthology of poems considered by the publishers to be the most beloved of every man, woman and child ever born or yet to be born within the United Kingdom and all her territories. It was the final word on the subject. Anybody who disagreed was either not really British or an out-and-out mental. Geoffrey hadn't actually heard of any of the poems within it, not having had a private education, and in six months of carrying it around with him had only found two that he even liked.

To use the same patronising reasoning that the book's publishers had employed, he must also have been a football fanatic, for, although he had never watched a professional match in his adult life, football was apparently a national obsession, and dog ownership practically compulsory!

Geoffrey had never been someone to get involved. 'What would've been the point?' he had asked himself. So he didn't agree with the publisher's 'informed' choices. He would've been pissing into a prevailing wind, the consequences of which were blindingly obvious to all involved, to have attempted to make a personal stand. They were bigger than he was and their opinions carried more clout.

It annoyed him, though. It wound him up, somewhere deep down inside him, in a hitherto untapped facet of his soul, a pan of resentment was bubbling over a fire of suppressed expression. Forsooth, but he hated poetry! Absorb enough of it and even your thought processes become camp and periphrastic!

He put the book down on the table in front of him, picked up his reinforced cardboard cup and supped at it. He had only tasted tea worse than this once before and that was when a student friend of his had put a teabag and a spoonful of sugar into a mug of cold water and milk and put it in a microwave to heat. He had tasted tea just as bad as this current offering, though. Yesterday. And the day before. Here. In this same . . . coffee shop.

He came here every morning, well, most mornings, whenever he was lucky enough to catch the early train and arrive in the city panic free. It was one of three identical coffeeshops that he had to pass, all operated by the same chain, between the station and his office. A choice of three. All the same. Same name, same layout, same menu and the same staff. Really? What, were they clones?

Why did they need three branches within a one-mile stretch, anyway? Choice, apparently, according to the blurb on the back of the menu 'more branches than anyone else gave their "guests" more choice'. Presumably the choice to stop here rather than there, to decide at precisely which moment in your journey to break for a cardboard cup full of brown cardboard liquid.

Once inside, however, your choices were boundless! Fourteen different varieties of coffee which, if so desired, could be blended with four separate types of milk. (What exactly is rice milk and how do you go about milking a grain of rice—or a hazelnut, for that matter?) They even had two kinds of sugar, a chemical sweetener and an organically sourced, vegan friendly, fair trade honey! That's three hundred and fifty corporate coffee combinations, if you're the kind of person who really gives a shit. They were, of course, it was tagged beneath their branded logo on everything from the napkins to the paper in the toilets in every single outlet. If you threw into the mix the fact that they served each of those options in a choice of three barely distinguishable cardboard cup sizes and had the option of adding a sprinkle of chocolate on each, that upped your options to three thousand possible combinations. And for the discerning weirdo they also offered (grudgingly) a quite staggering range of twenty-five different blends of tea! Except that they didn't. It was the same 'English Breakfast' teabag, just served in twenty-five combinations with or without milk and/or sugar/honey. And it tasted horrible! It had always tasted horrible, yet he had always drunk it (milk and brown sugar) because his only other choice would have been no tea at all.

'The Nation's Favourite Coffee Shop' it read, just above the name and the strapline. Geoffrey had never noticed that before. 'Which nation?' he thought. 'This nation?' It wasn't an English company, they were an American franchise, so whose decision had that been? Had a poll been taken, preferences put forward and voted upon? And where had he been that day, as nobody had consulted him? He was a member of this nation and he was a regular customer of this chain, so why hadn't they asked him? He knew what he would have said if they had, though and it took him quite by surprise as he realised.

'Excuse me,' he said to the off-the-shelf assistant behind the counter wearing the lobotomised face, 'but is there any reason why this tea has to taste so . . . shit?'

'It's a coffeeshop, sir,' the assistant replied without blinking.

'. . . and?' Geoffrey pressed, thirty years' worth of unexpressed opinion rising to the fore.

'We serve coffee, sir. We have three thousand special blends, would you like to try one, sir?'

'You have fourteen, actually and no, thank you, I prefer tea.'

'Would you like to try a different tea, sir? We serve twenty-five different—'

'No you don't, you serve *one* type of tea! Albeit in twenty-five different colour-coded cardboard cups.'

Geoffrey took a breath. Rage was not his natural state. 'So I ask you again . . . Julie,' he said, suddenly clocking her 'Hi, I'm Julie, grunt at me, trainee assistant manager!' name badge, 'why is your tea so shit?'

'It's a regional concession,' she eventually replied, as if waiting for the answer to be downloaded from a central database of stock answers. 'Our parent chain in the States don't stock tea at all.'

'Oh,' said Geoffrey, contemplating the fit of his new personality, 'so you're actually doing me a favour by serving me shit tea, then?'

They hadn't needed to ban him from every one of their twelve million branches worldwide, Geoffrey had already made the decision himself that he would never set foot in one again. As the squad responsible for subduing anarchist uprisings loaded him into the back of their van, Geoffrey quietly considered his options. He decided to hand in his notice . . . and open a teashop.

19

Insignificant Other

He'd been a long time dead, now. So long gone, in fact, that very few people still remembered that he'd ever been here at all. His mother thought of him fleetingly, occasionally, but they hadn't seen each other for years, so there really hadn't been much for her to miss, coupled with the fact that she suffered from Alzheimer's and usually couldn't even remember who she was.

He'd had friends, of course, most people do, and they'd raised a glass to him at his wake, but then they'd moved on with their lives. New faces had joined their circle bringing with them new interests and new ideas. And even the places that he had once frequented with them had changed: a renovation here, a restoration there, there was very little left now to tie his memory to. Time waits for no man, especially a dead one.

His girlfriend had thought about him more than most. She had *had* to. It had been left to her to organise his funeral and she had also inherited the morbid task of sorting his few remaining possessions and disposing of the remnants of his life. She had shed a tear or two at the time, but if you want to know the truth, his passing had been more of a relief to her than it had been a shock. It wasn't that he had been suffering a painful and protracted illness and that his passing had been a welcome blessing, no, he had been in rude health right up to the moment when the blade had pierced his heart, but the tears hadn't been for him in any case.

They had been tears of guilt. Guilt, because although they had been living as a couple for just shy of two years, she hadn't loved him. She may have done once, way back when it had all begun, but she couldn't really remember *why* she might have thought that and whatever it may have been that had attracted her to him in the first place had long since worn away like the patch of carpet in front of the chair where he had so often sat poring over his bloody notes and diagrams.

His sudden violent death had been quite convenient for her actually, as it had saved her the awkwardness of having to ask him to leave. The last time that she had thought of him had been as she had been dropping a box of his old photographs and paperwork into a skip at her local tip.

As she had been removing her gloves and returning to her car she had bumped into a man with whom she would go on to have a passionate affair, marry and later have four children with, which was ironic because she had never even wanted children when she had been with him. She had forgotten this, though, as easily as she had forgotten him, before she had even made it home.

Curiously, the one person left in the world who did still think of him from time to time was the person who knew him the least well of all: his murderer. They had only met briefly the once, well, when I say *met* it wasn't in the traditional sense of meeting someone.

There was no exchange of pleasantries nor shaking of hands, in fact neither knew the other's name until after the killer's subsequent arrest. It had all been so casual and cheap—no names, no conversation, just two men briefly sharing the same spot in time and space, looking to any who might have been watching like lovers in an embrace, two men greeting each other in that time-honoured fashion as knife-wielder and victim. He thought about him now and again, he wondered who he was and what his final thought might have been, wondered whether what he'd done that day had had any real impact on the general fabric of the universe.

No he didn't. I made that last bit up! In the ten years that he'd spent incarcerated he hadn't *once* considered the consequences of that day's selfish actions.

He had chosen his victim entirely at random. When questioned at his trial he hadn't been able to recall what it had been about that particular man that had made him want to stab him. He hadn't 'looked at him funny', he hadn't caused him any particular offence. He hadn't been wearing anything that might've marked him out as 'asking for it' in any way. He had just been, in his killer's psychotic opinion, 'an insignificant other'—someone nobody'd miss.

And that had always been his problem. Nobody had *ever* really noticed him, well, except for his killer, and he'd only noticed him because he wasn't very noticeable. Instantly forgettable. Perhaps the ideal face for a stalker or a spy. But he hadn't been either.

He had been a scientist, and a hardworking one at that, which is probably why he'd spent so little time with his friends and family over the years. He had been working on a formula when he had been so arbitrarily executed on his way to the patent office. He had been about to register a genetic recoding sequence that would halt the ageing process in human beings, meaning that no one need ever grow old and die again. His satchel containing the memory card which held his encrypted formulae had not been recovered from the crime scene. He had left his paper notes including evidence of all of the experiments that had led to the discovery in a locked drawer in his girlfriend's spare room, along with a series of photographs of his test subjects as back-up, just in case his computer ever chose to let him down.

But for that unfortunate meeting, both *his* fate and ultimately that of the human race itself would have been very different. However, as an addendum, it's worth mentioning that, had he *not* died so suddenly and had his formula been acted upon, his girlfriend *would* have remembered what it was that she had loved about him in the first place and they would have had a son together. Years later in response to his father's legacy—a world so overcrowded that in order to combat international food shortages the population had turned to cannibalism—the budding scientist would create and release a pathogen that wiped out all life on earth.

Sometimes it's probably best just to let fate have her way.

20

The 65ers

Day 1

Well what else was I supposed to do, eh? I needed a job. I had bills to pay and I'm not exactly anybody's Einstein. I'm a soldier. It's all I've ever known. I know my place, I believe in the chain of command and I follow orders without question. Life was easy in the Army, except when people were trying to kill me. But even then I knew how things worked. There was a protocol for everything. I didn't have to think about it. I wasn't being paid to think. Thinking's not what soldiers do.

That's why they give you a uniform and a buzz cut. It's to save you from yourself, to save you from having to make decisions.

Day 2

As a soldier you need to be able to react with lightning speed and pinpoint precision. Lives often depend on it. If I'd ever stopped to debate the moral, ethical or spiritual implications of an order before carrying it out then I would probably not be sitting here today considering the moral, ethical and spiritual ramifications of taking a job with the Civil Service.

And breaking that kind of conditioning isn't easy, either. You'd think we'd want to, wouldn't you, that our human spirit would be desperate to reassert itself as soon as the opportunity arose? But as anyone who's ever seen a formation of off-duty squaddies on their way to their local pub of an evening will attest, 'casual' is no longer the default setting of the initiated.

So I was used to donning the kit and doing as I was told. I didn't have a problem with boxing my emotions and toeing the line for Queen an' country or 'The Greater Good', if that was the campaign's tagline this week.

Or so I had thought.

Day 3

When I'd been interviewed for the position of 'loss adjuster', I had naively presumed this to be some kind of 'office-speak' jargon for debt collector. I thought I was being hired more for my physical prowess than my army skills: y'know, the sight of a stocky, shaven-headed professional thug on your doorstep having a more immediate effect than a brace of final demands and court orders ever would. Several of my ex-platoon mates had gone into this line, if not nightclub bouncing then private security, once they had decided that getting blown up and shot at for a living wasn't quite the arcade game that we'd all expected it to be. Any of the above would have been a safer way of earning a living and a career with greater long-term prospects. People would always need to be roughed up and threatened with violence, but to be able to do it to people who weren't armed with Kalashnikovs and plastic explosives was a positive plus. However, the unit that I found myself assigned to after accepting the post and signing a copy of the Official Secrets Act (the document that I am now defying, if only in my personal diary) was anything but a gang of burly government bailiffs on the hunt for the odd benefit fraudster and small-time tax evader.

Day 4

They call themselves the 65ers, although their official title is the Pensions and Welfare Office. They are a top secret organisation housed in an old wartime bunker adjacent to the Piccadilly line. There are five of us in the unit: Commander Barton, ex SAS and on permanent loan from MI6, a psycho reject from Special Branch who we only know as 'Fruit Cake' who acts as our sergeant, and three ex-front line grunts: myself, 'Spaz' McGurk and Toby Ironside. I'm the new boy. Everybody else was recruited, but they had recently lost one of their own when a mission had gone wrong and had been having some trouble finding a replacement. Hence the subtle subterfuge involved in my own recruitment.

The 65ers don't show up on any list of covert government agencies. They don't officially exist and if word ever got out that they did then there would be riots in the towns and cities of this once fair and free country of ours, of a like never before seen this side of a civil war. There isn't much in the England of the twenty-first century that would rile the citizenship to the extent that they would take their grievances to the streets en masse—most British people are happy just to tut and moan over a few jars about the injustices that are now routinely inflicted on them by a ruling elite so removed from the lives of the ordinaries as to be, in essence, an entirely different species. But this is different.

Day 5

We receive our orders directly from someone called the 'Minister', which could be a code name for all that I've managed to ascertain, but could equally well refer to a member of the Cabinet. And when I say orders, I do of course mean targets. For that's what this top secret black ops unit really is: we're a hit squad, an assassination team. We deal with the 'trouble' elements in today's society.

I should be used to killing. It's what I do best. Target the enemy, pull the trigger: end his life. For Queen an' country. For the Greater Good. No feelings = No regrets. Orders are orders. They know what they're doing, they have their reasons. I'm just an instrument. My conscience is clear.

But this . . .

Maybe I'm getting soft. Maybe it's the fact that this unit is plainclothes. Or maybe it's the fact that what we do here is just wrong. I don't know why I'm letting it get to me like this. I'm a soldier. I should be able to detach myself from the reality of it. Perhaps I've been reading too much since I've been out of barracks.

Day 6

A soldier's pay is really quite basic, especially given the inherent danger associated with the job. The 65ers, however, are another story. We're technically civil servants, with a pay scale and the perks to go with it. Our salary is designed to take into account the fact that this job is not only objectionable but also not without its risks.

Day 7

Silent Eddie, the guy that I replaced, didn't die in the line of fire. He didn't suffer a fatal industrial accident or get shot by his own side. Silent Eddie is doing life for murder. Y'see, we don't exactly have a licence to kill. If we get caught going about our day-to-day business by members of any of our sister services, we are held personally accountable for our actions. An assassination becomes a murder and the Minister and his accomplices further up the chain deny all knowledge of our existence and feed the press with the standard and all too plausible 'civil servant runs amok' line. It's a precarious profession, but it's also the reason why a lowly civil servant such as myself is able to drive a Jaguar XJS.

Day 8

It seems that somebody upstairs is developing a conscience. Either that or they're worried that the British economy isn't able to support this unit's generous pay deal in the face of ever increasing life expectancy. The statutory retirement age has just been raised to sixty-eight and will gradually rise to seventy over the next few years. I'm not sure if that's going to make this job easier or harder. Statistically that will leave us with fewer targets, but it also means that we will be arranging the 'accidental deaths' of even older people, people for whom the promise of a restful retirement after the better part of their lives have been spent in servitude to the system, has been cruelly stolen from them in order that the machine may squeeze that final drop of life from them in the hope that our services need not be required.

Try as I might, I am having a great deal of trouble convincing myself that these people pose a threat to our collective national interests. I know, I know, I shouldn't try to out-think the brass. They know what they're doing. Mine is not to question. But it'd be so much easier if they at least spoke a different language, or were of a different colour or religion to myself.

Day 9

This is like shooting your granddad in the back because you've outgrown his anecdotes. My task today, should I choose to accept it, and of course I must as it is an order, not a request, is to arrange a fatal gardening accident for a Mr Harold Goodman, sixty-five, of 15 Railway Cuttings. Harold used to be a florist. He's led quite an innocuous life, according to his file. He's always paid his bills on time, he's never made a claim for any benefit of any kind and has always voted Conservative, even during the John Major years. In 1982 he wrote a letter to his local paper bemoaning the fact that people who let their dogs foul the pavements should be sent to Russia to 'see how they liked it'. Hardly a dissenter. But then, targets aren't necessarily chosen for their radicalisation.

England is broken. The situation is far worse than people believe. People are living longer than they were ever expected to live when the great betting scam that we call National Insurance was first floated. Too many people are living past sixty-five. Too many people are living too long into their retirement and claiming back the money that they were promised, but which the government has squandered, keeping lowlifes like me in regular employment overseas.

Has nobody ever questioned the fact that a conspicuous number of people seem to die in this country within a year of retirement? Take my advice, Harold. Get a part-time job in a garden centre. Quick. Keep paying your taxes. Because the moment you stop to tend your roses, that's when you'll get a visit from the 65ers.

21

Experience Required

He had contemplated suicide, well, let's face it, who hasn't at some point in their life? He hadn't planned to throw himself under a train nor anything so melodramatic, he'd just idly wondered one day whether it was something he might be likely to consider, you know, if things ever got that bad, if he ever found himself unable to see his way out of a situation. And that was why he had the perspective that he had now, how he knew just how far he would go. It was how he gauged life's little risks, chose when to stay and when to go. It's called a Self-Preservation Instinct and we all have one. We'd be dead without it.

So be honest: who hasn't rolled the idea around in their heads at least once and asked themselves the ultimate question: 'How much does being alive actually mean to me?'

Simon had answered that question a long time ago. Life, to him, meant everything, staying alive—his imperative. Life wasn't something he took for granted. It hadn't been something he'd asked for, it'd been given to him freely, and what more precious a gift could be given than the gift of life? If his mother hadn't have been quite so pissed that night and his father spoken enough English to have understood the word 'no', then he might never have been conceived and, of course, he would never have been any the wiser, but since he *had* been, he was going to make damn sure that he made the most of it.

A happy accident, then, as his mother had always called him, and that about summed it all up for Simon. All life was a happy accident, if you thought about it, wasn't it? Nothing had ever willed itself into existence. Nobody had ever demanded to be born.

Some people see life as a burden, a great heavy weight that has been foisted upon them. They feel a pressure to 'make something of themselves', to prove their worth amongst all the other happy accidents, to fulfil what they see as their . . . 'destiny'. Simon wasn't one of them. To Simon it wasn't about making a mark, to Simon it was about experiencing everything that was out there to be experienced.

So he took risks, of course he did.

If you never took risks then you might as well just sit in an armchair all day staring at the back of your eyelids! But Simon didn't take risks for the sake of taking risks, oh, no. His risks were calculated risks, odds-contemplated-in-advance-type risks. He wanted to live to risk again! That was that old self-preservation instinct of his: never take a risk unless the potential gain from taking said risk is something that you can't possibly live without.

And all of that had held true for Simon for the first twenty-nine years of his life and although he still believed as he had always believed, the adventures he now sought were greater and the risk factor involved, far less predictable than ever before.

He wanted to see the world, did Simon, to explore uncharted environments, to encounter unknown cultures and to experience every strange, new sensation that he could. Simon wanted to do everything. The more he did, the more he wanted to do, the further he went, the further he needed to go, but the greater the experience, as he had recently come to realise, the more expensive its acquisition. Which is how he had come to find himself experiencing the same things over and over again in order to save enough moolah to escape.

Then, one day, he saw the answer, staring up at him from his newspaper: 'Twenty-year-old art student auctions her virginity online for a hundred and fifty thousand pounds.'

Now, it was a little late for that in his case, and besides, what woman would want to buy a boy's virginity? Not very likely. But it was the principle that had caught his eye. Just as people were prepared to pay for a unique, once-in-a-lifetime experience, so too was it possible to *sell* an experience. And if you sold something that you had never done before, then you could experience whilst also profiteering! It was perfect.

Simon put an advert in Exchange & Mart: 'EXPERIENCES REQUIRED, ALL OFFERS CONSIDERED.'

He was open for pretty much anything, he'd decided.

The first few calls to come in had been from weirdos with dungeons and bondage fetishes. That was to be expected, he'd supposed.

He'd listened to their offers, but had already done everything that they'd wanted to do to him and hadn't found it particularly thrilling or addictive the first time around. He had a request from a man who wanted to know what it was like to eat someone and was looking for someone who wanted to know what it would be like to be eaten. Although the idea of experiencing the Ultimate Experience was a fascinating one, he couldn't see how the person being eaten would get anything out of the transaction. He decided to pass on that one too.

A week later he received another call. Would he like to sell a kidney? No, he wouldn't. The following day another request, again of a medical nature: had he ever considered drug trials?

For three thousand pounds he could allow himself to be infected with a non-fatal virus. He would be kept in a secure, luxury environment for four weeks whilst being treated with either an experimental cure or a placebo while the drug's manufacturers studied his rate of recovery and, presumably, any side-effects that might manifest themselves.

Well that didn't sound so bad, thought Simon. He weighed the potential risk against the financial outcome and considered the experience. Why not?

As experiences went it was a little dull, but it'd given him the chance to read up on a few places he'd like to visit and it had been well paid.

A week later he received another call from the same source.

Would he be interested in furthering the cause of medical science by undertaking a minor surgical procedure? Not another kidney request, he wondered? It wasn't. They wanted to remove a finger. Cut it off and stitch it back on again. For ten grand. At first the idea turned his stomach, but then, the more he thought about it, the more the thought of the experience itself began to intrigue him. He remembered reading an article some years back about a climber who had amputated his own hand with a penknife after becoming trapped halfway up a mountain. It wasn't a predicament that he would have been eager to copy, but the thought of the experience had opened new pathways within his mind, expanded his processes with a new conundrum. Just how far *was* he prepared to go to feel something new?

They had assured him that the risks were minimal. It was by no means the first time that they had carried out the procedure and it would be conducted under controlled medical conditions. He mulled the opportunity over for a couple of days, but as with their previous request, Simon found that he just couldn't resist . . . the *experience*.

It was a couple of months until he was able to fully use his little finger again, but apart from a hairline scar and a minor lessening of sensitivity along one side, he appeared to have suffered no permanent ill effect. And he was ten grand up.

It was some time before he received another call, but receive it he eventually would.

Would he be interested in furthering the blah blah blah by allowing the waffle waffle waffle to put him to sleep by halting the function of his heart and then to revive him using an experimental—woah, woah, woah! Put-him-to-sleep? The oft-used euphemism much bantered by vets? Would he be prepared to die, just for the experience (and one hundred and fifty thousand pounds) if he knew that they could bring him back again? There was very little risk, they once again assured him, it was all scientifically controlled, but they would have to insist that he made out a will, this time, before signing on the dotted line.

He wouldn't be dead for long.

Some people had out of body experiences during their brief spells unalive, they saw bright lights and angels or saw their bodies as if they were floating above them, looking down.

How far was too far to go for an experience of a lifetime? Was he prepared to take the ultimate risk for the ultimate experience?

He thought about it. It was a lot of money. He could gain a lot of experiences with that much money. If he really wanted he could even buy the virginity of a twenty-year-old art student! Risk his life for something that most people are desperate to get rid of for free . . .

Yes, he'd considered it. I'm sure we all have at some time or other. It's a useful marker, you see.

Contemplating extremes is often the only time that we stop to look at the details.

Simon decided that it was about time he tried out some of life's more mundane experiences. For free.

22

The Shoes Made Me Do It

Toby was a sensitive man, he didn't mind admitting it. He always had been. Not that sensitivity was something to be ashamed of these days, God no! The world had matured over the past few years, these were liberated times we were living in. Just as female emancipation and the advent of the birth control pill had given women the chance to take control of their lives, so too it had given men the chance to grow, freed from the shackles of the need to put brawn before brain in an alpha-dominated race to procreate. Girls liked a softer man nowadays, someone as adept at comforting a crying child in the middle of the night as he was at putting up a shelf in the bathroom or fending off a burglar with a cricket bat. Toby was a 'New Man', in touch with his feminine side, not afraid to show emotion, unembarrassed to admit to pacifism, veganism and the occasional use of a little foundation, just under the eyes to hide his bags.

His mother had warned him about showing too much emotion.

'All this New Age empathy lark's going to get you into trouble one day, my lad,' she had said. 'You jus' see if it don't!'

But Toby just couldn't help himself. He'd been known to cry at slushy films and got so overwhelmed at the pictures of animals in distress that constantly flowed through his letterbox, sent by manipulative charities who knew him to have been a soft touch with other manipulative charities with whom they traded mailing lists, that he was no longer even able to open them, instead passing them straight through his shredder rather than falling for their heartstring-tugging tactics again and again.

Toby was the kind of man who, when stepping over the threshold into a building that he had never been into before, instantly seemed to absorb whatever intense emotional residue had been left behind by the structure's previous residents.

This tended to manifest itself as either a feeling of heightened euphoria or of claustrophobic foreboding. He called it his sixth sense. It worked on people too, though he suspected that that may have had as much to do with a person's innate natural ability to read body language and pheromone markers as it did his sensitivity toward esoteric trace emotions.

Weird. He had a feeling he was going to have this feeling about this particular house long before he had even stepped onto the mat and it hadn't disappointed him. He'd had this feeling before, once, years back, when he'd been flat-hunting for the first time. It was actually very hard to explain. Sceptics who might try to rationalise away such supernatural abilities, often put them down to sudden shifts in room temperature to which some people are naturally more sensitive than others. But fluctuating temperatures had nothing to do with it. It wasn't what the place made *him* feel: his own mood was surprisingly untainted by the effect. It felt more like a leftover feeling of someone else's that had been so strong that it lingered on long after they had gone. Was that even possible? He thought so and he had been proven right before.

Something bad had happened in this house, just as it had in that flat above the butcher's shop that he had thankfully chosen not to rent before being told about the murders that had taken place there.

He shouldn't even have been here. Technically he had just broken and entered, if it counts as breaking and entering if one uses the key that one found under a plant pot in the garden, that is. This sixth sense of his had been working overtime. He didn't

know this house, he had no idea who lived here, he had just felt
. . . compelled to come here, wherever here was, as if someone or
something had been reaching out to him, calling him here.

As he'd opened the front door it had hit him, just as strongly as
if he had been hit in the face by a New Man's cricket bat.

Pain. Pain and . . . fear.

He was standing in somebody's living room. He knew he
shouldn't be here: he had no right to be here but the impulse had
overwhelmed him.

It had started yesterday on a lunch-hour excursion into town,
when he had dropped into his favourite charity shop. He always
called in when he had a spare couple of minutes. You never knew
what you might find in a second-hand shop and best of all, you
attained the feeling that your impulsive and frivolous purchase
was going some way towards helping someone in greater need
than yourself, rather than just satiating your own lust for
acquisition, the antithesis to the feeling of suicidal desperation
that so overpowered the supermarket shopping experience. He
had bought himself a pair of shoes. Nothing special, but save for
a couple of scuff-marks on the backs which he'd felt sure would
polish out, they'd been too good to pass. Once or twice in the past
he had had a 'feeling' about an item that had caught his eye.
Usually a melancholia, as if the previous owner had been reluctant
to part with an 'old friend'. The moment he had put these shoes
on, however, he had been assaulted by the same intense emotional
barrage that had hit him as he had entered what he had taken to
be their previous owner's home. Ridiculous, he knew, but there
was no other explanation for why he had come here. The shoes
had made him do it!

It was an ordinary room in an ordinary house, but its very
substance was screaming out in terror. It was in the walls, it was
in the furniture, it was in the disturbed motes of airborne dust as
he passed through them. Someone had died in here, someone had
died in this room. No . . . not someone: one person's death would
surely not have left such a strong impression. *Many* people had

died here. Yes, he could feel that now. Many . . . sensitive people had been drawn here, drawn here to die! He could almost hear their silent screams as he began to panic, fear-laced sweat dripping from his body, soaking into his socks and pooling in his new shoes. He heard the front door close behind him and two internal bolts being pulled and slammed into place. Toby turned slowly, his heart pounding as that damnable sixth sense absorbed the anger and the hatred emanating from the man who he had correctly guessed to be standing behind him . . . holding a bloodied cricket bat . . .

Epilogue
Toby was a sensitive man in a world where sensitivity often got one into trouble. Or killed, if you were daft enough to let those sensitivities get the better of you. Toby, however, may have been sensitive, but he was not a weak man and he knew how to make his emotions work for him, how to channel the fear and the pain into instruments of anger and revenge. They'd just been an ordinary pair of shoes to the average passer-by, but in the right hands, or on the right feet, they had the power of every man who had ever died in them . . . in that room.

Except the last one.

Toby swapped shoes with his victim, the shoes that had kicked the man to death, just to baffle the police.

23

Careless Talk Costs Wives

She was a good listener, people had always said so: easy to talk to. She had an honest face. She never pried or tried to draw more information than was being freely proffered and she wasn't a gossip. Not like the others. People instinctively knew that they could trust Tracy, in that way that her parent's generation had grown up with that unquestioning belief in the integrity of the British beat 'bobby'. They trusted her as she had once been encouraged to trust her priest with the embarrassing yearnings of her pubescent mind. Yes, that was the analogy that best befitted her talents, the irony lost to her clients, thankfully. She was a professional confessional.

She really had no idea why people chose to invest quite so much faith in her as the guardian of their guiltiest secrets rather than confide in their closest friends or their families, surely it couldn't possibly be something as simple as a fortuitous bone structure or her Catholic schooling?

There was no Hippocratic oath to govern the wagging tongues of her particular trade. Perhaps they sensed a kindred spirit in the way that she absorbed their gory tales of domestic strife with her trademarked brand of tea and sympathy, never appearing to doubt the abject veracity of their stories and never offering unsolicited advice nor allowing herself to slander the pantomime villains of the piece to their distraught spouses.

Perhaps it was this air of presumed neutrality that made her such a popular sounding-board, who can say?

And it wasn't a contrived persona. She had never actively invited people to unburden themselves on her. This wasn't something that she sought as a means of financial gain, nor was she intending to use her ladies' collected woes as stakes in a coffeebreak game of hearsay poker: the most outlandish tale of marital misery that morning winning its teller a turn-out of the washing-up duties. No. Tracy was different and her ladies knew this. 'You radiate a natural aura of serene sagacity,' she had once been told, whatever that meant, and it had always been the same for her. During her teens she had often found herself the unwilling confidante to one or other or even both of her sparring parents, neither believing for a second that her loyalty to their cause could ever be compromised, it was just accepted as being a part of who she was. But there was an inherent problem that came with being everybody else's shoulder-to-cry-on and that was that there was never anybody available for her when she needed an ear.

Tracy never talked about herself. She was a very private person. She had opinions, but she never voiced them publicly. She never tried to dominate a conversation. She merely allowed them to unload, to talk through their problems until they came to their own conclusions. She listened. A cynic might have accused her of not really caring, of not doing enough to help her ladies, of being more interested in their generous tips than their tribulations, but that cynic would have been wrong.

And anyway, what if that were true? It wasn't as if she was a therapist or anything. She was only their hairdresser.

Mrs Stevens' husband had been brutally murdered two weeks ago. It had been a terrible shock to everyone, not least of all to Mrs Stevens herself, who, all this time later, was still prone to blub whenever anyone tried to speak to her. He had been the unfortunate victim of what the police were calling a 'blundered mugging', according to the three inches of typeface that The Daily Rumour had been able to spare him under the headline 'VIOLENT CRIME ON THE UP'. He had been on his way home from work when his attacker had struck him from behind with a single slash of a cutthroat razor. In broad daylight, too! He had barely been two hundred yards from his own front door.

His assailant had escaped with a worthless forgery of a wristwatch, which had been discarded in a hedge in the next street and a paltry fifty pounds in cash. The police were treating the incident as a statistic. Nobody had come forward with any information and the body had been released for burial.

Mrs Stevens' attitude toward the news of her philandering husband's frankly overdue demise had taken Tracy quite by surprise, having listened for the previous nine months to the tales of his suspected misdeeds. She had seen her arrive for her weeklies, red-eyed and less than made-up and had watched through her mirror as she had sat on the reception sofa snuffling her way through a box of tissues while awaiting her stylist's ministrations.

She had listened sympathetically while the poor wretch had spewed forth her lists of late meetings, delayed trains and team-building exercises in the Lake District that had often required him to be away from home for the length of time commonly required for a 'dirty weekend'. She had plenty of theories. He had been employing the rather convenient and some would say pathetic 'mid-life crisis' excuse for his lack of nocturnal interest and this had been the catalyst that had sent his long-suffering wife spinning through her spiral of conspiracy and mistrust. It was an old story and Tracy had heard it more times than she cared to remember. She hadn't seen any proof, no carelessly undeleted emails or details of regularly called, yet unlisted numbers, but as ever, she had taken the menopausal housewife at her word none the less. She saw it every day. It was as common as the clap to an enthusiastic audience. Fifteen years on the floor had taught her a thing or two about middle-aged men. And what was proof anyway? Proof just meant that a man had been sloppy enough to let himself get caught out. It was when you didn't have proof that you needed to worry! They were the ones to watch! Knowing what your man was getting up to when he wasn't with you was one thing, but *not* knowing for certain whilst having a good idea of what *other* men did was enough to break a woman's sanity! Oh, he had been guilty all right. She just didn't know what of.

So when the aforementioned Mrs Stevens was still bursting into floods at the backwash all those weeks later, Tracy found herself at a loss to prescribe her usual platitudes.

It reminded her of the way politicians spent all day slagging one another off with poshly worded insults whilst referring to one another as 'the honorable gentleman, or lady'. She didn't know why, it just did.

Perhaps it was misplaced guilt? Maybe a previously boxed memory of the couple's earlier, happier times together had been prised open by the shock of it all. Or was she for some reason regretting not turning a blind eye to his extramarital indiscretions, blaming herself for insisting that he come straight home that night to sit with his loopy mother so that she could attend her yoga class on time for a change? Tracy found herself completely unable to comfort her client in her usual way. She found herself irritated by the woman's constant sobbing and snuffling and all the little involuntary movements of the head that went with them as she deployed her entire patience reserve in attempting to roll her wet hair around little plastic curlers. The man who had caused his wife so much pain and misery was dead. She was free at last. She ought to be grateful to his murderer, well . . . maybe that was a bit strong, but she should at least have felt relieved that her torture was over.

Tracy had never really understood human relationships, it was fair to say. Oh, her clients saw her as an expert, lauding her natural talent for marriage guidance, but nobody had ever considered how little personal experience she actually had on the subject. Truth be revealed, she had never had a relationship herself, not unless you counted her cats, but that was a different dynamic entirely. Her cats never gave her any grief.

Cats were also good listeners and they took whatever they were told to the grave with them.

She'd had no shortage of offers, mind, over the years, but she'd spurned every last one of them. It was all too messy and too complicated for her. She had watched her parent's relationship disintegrate and die throughout her adolescence, heard the once loving couple who had fought so hard to bring her into the world bawl ever more venomous insults over her head. She had lived the pain with them and had decided then not to try it for herself. And every time that she had been forced to listen to yet another heartbroken wife she had had that decision further vindicated.

Why would you put yourself through all that, she wondered, practically daily.

It was always going to end badly for one of you. If they didn't cheat, beat or lie to you they'd eventually die on you. She didn't believe in happy endings. She shuddered at the thought as she placed the hood-dryer over the simpering Mrs Stevens and cranked the heat dial up to 4. Why did they do it to themselves? They should spend a day in her shoes. They'd see all the examples they needed to keep them single for the rest of their sorry lives!

Tracy checked her watch. It was one of those upside-down ones that pinned to her overall like the ones nurses used to wear. She saw her four o'clock out of the corner of her eye as she waddled into reception, bang on time as usual. In the fifteen years of setting Mrs Batts at four o'clock every Wednesday she couldn't recall her ever having been late. Shame some of her other regulars couldn't follow her example. Mrs Batts was her favourite. She was a sweet old dear. Always chirpy, always pleased to see everyone and never a bad word for anyone. And she always brought a little bunch of flowers from her shop to brighten the salon. She was her little ray of sunshine. After the wrist-slittingly depressing fifteen minutes that she'd just spent with the ever mournful Mrs Stevens she felt her spirits rise as she moved to intercept her longest running client. Skye, Tracy's part-time receptionist, didn't feel quite the same way about the retired florist. Skye had always maintained that there was something odd about Edna Batts, and she should know: she was supposed to have been a bit psychic. 'It's in the eyes,' she'd said, 'something's not quite kosher, there.'

A couple of weeks back, at Tara's hen party, and after a substantial soaking of Malibu, Skye had tried to convince everyone that dear, sweet Mrs Batts was in fact The Rumour's notorious 'Pedestrian Slayer', even though Barry Ogilvy, that creepy taxi driver who always used to leer at her when he passed her at the bus stop had already been arrested for that particular murder spree. As soon as Skye had heard the news about Mr Stevens she'd been straight on the phone to point the finger of blame. Okay, so paranoia was understandably rife, at the moment. There had been an unusually large number of unsolved and grisly murders in the area over the past few years. Everyone had been hoping that with Ogilvy's arrest people might have started feeling a little safer, but the police had only managed to pin a handful of the victims on her former classmate. There was another killer at large, that much was obvious, but Tracy just knew it wasn't Edna Batts.

She waited while Skye helped the old lady out of her rain mac' and into a spot-bleached nylon gown, dropping the coat onto a hanger as if its touch might contaminate her fingertips. She pulled a face behind her back as she escorted her through to the backwash as if she were leading her to the gallows.

'Your four o'clock, Tracy, love,' she said, before silently mouthing the word 'killer' for only Tracy to see. Tracy admonished her with a stern grimace and called for her apprentice Fleur to break out the shampoo.

There was 'something' about Edna, though.

In the fifteen years of setting that same head, week in, week out, she realised how little she had actually discovered about her. Tracy wasn't a pryer, that wasn't her style at all. She had never needed to be. Her ladies tended to disgorge their innermost within minutes of a good detangling, whether she wanted them to or not, but dear old Edna Batts had always been more interested in other people's lives than her own. Funny that. Funny that she'd never noticed that before. She owned the florist on the corner of St Kitts Street and she played bingo on a Wednesday evening. That was it. That was as personal as she had ever got. The florist was run by a man of about the same age, whom Tracy had always 'presumed' to have been Edna's husband, but she couldn't recall her ever 'saying' so.

They could have been siblings, even, or it could quite feasibly have been a purely professional arrangement. Tracy decided to try a little subtle conversational manipulation, purely in the interests of being in a better position to support her client's good character, of course, but as Fleur led the dripping pensioner across to her workstation, she noticed something unusual about her. It was as if she had lived a year's span in the space of a week. Tracy helped her into her adjustable chair and removed her towelling turban, noting the run-marks in her caked foundation where the ditzy junior had carelessly allowed water to drip into her ears and down her neck. And there were similar marks in the make-up beneath her eyes: dried tear tracts in the furrows of her face, if she wasn't mistaken, and she knew that she wasn't.

She'd seen this a thousand times before. Had she perhaps overheard Skye's ludicrous accusations or had Fleur's ridiculously impractical false nails tortured yet another frail old dear whilst she had supposedly been giving them a soothing scalp massage?

She began with her usual generic platitudes and enquiries as to her client's general welfare, but received nothing in return, save for a painfully strained smile. She combed her hair back from her face, applied a generous dollop of mousse and attempted to draw the old lady into conversation. Again she was answered with nothing more than a slight upward twist of the lips. Tracy was annoyed with herself. Why was it that when she couldn't give a monkey's toss about the intricacies of someone's squalid little life then they couldn't unload it quickly enough, but when for once she did actually find herself really caring about someone, they clammed up like a nun at a charity gangbang! She hated a mystery. She knew what men were capable of and she knew that she could help. She prided herself on the fact that she probably knew more about the ins and outs of this neighbourhood than anybody else did, and that included that weird 'watcher' bloke in the flats who never moved from his window all day!

'And what about Mr Batts?' she suddenly blurted, instantly chastising herself for her junior detective bluntness by jabbing herself with the steel tail of her comb. Stupid, stupid, she silently admonished as the old lady's eyes began to wrinkle in on themselves as if preparing to wring another round of tears from their ducts.

Her lips began to quiver, but she sniffed back her pain and battled to contain her emotion. Even Skye would have been subtler, and everyone knew what she did to supplement her income! It was the kind of basic mistake more commonly made by young Fleur with her bottle-blonde savvy and her estate gob.

'He's . . . ,' she faltered warily, as if Tracy had suddenly become a stranger to her. 'He's okay, thanks. And your cats?'

Tracy breathed a sigh of relief. She had got away with her amateur faux pas. She caught sight of Skye in the mirror mouthing 'she killed him' and drawing a finger across her throat to represent the modus operandi of Mrs Steven's husband's murderer. Tracy glared menacingly back at her, but caught sight of an incredulous Fleur at the backwash mouthing 'really??' at Skye.

Oh, for a better class of staff.

'They're fine,' she replied, pulling her roller-trolley closer and preparing to wind. 'Would you like a tissue?' she asked gently.

'Thank you, dear. I don't know where that came from.'

'Fleur?' called Tracy. 'Cuppa tea, two sugars and don't forget the saucer!'

She rested a pair of hairpins between over-rouged lips.

'Are you . . . ,' she stuttered, 'have you . . . has someone . . . ?'

She stared through the mirror at her snuffling client. Where her make-up had run, two purple shiners were now quite visible.

'I'm so sorry,' the old lady blurted, her eyes welling up once more.

'D'you think she needs some brandy in it?' asked Fleur, slapping the mug down in front of her. Tracy glared at her as Mrs Batts finally released the floodgates. She picked up her handbag, shrugged her way out of her gown and tottered off into the street without even stopping to collect her mac.

'Guilt,' mouthed both Skye and Fleur in unison.

Two Wednesdays at four o'clock passed with no sign of Edna Batts. On the second she decided to act. It was always the quiet ones whose lives were the most miserable. The poor old dear had probably been suffering for decades at that man's hands. He was obviously a drinker. She had guessed that much from her reaction to Fleur's innocent but stupid attempt to spice her tea with the brandy that they always kept in the staffroom to calm the brides.

She closed up early that night, having seen the ever whinging Loretta Stevens out at 4:30 and allowing the girls an early night. She pulled down the blinds and walked through to the back of the shop, through the beaded arch and into the staffroom. The more upmarket high street salons had computers to keep their client records on, but Tracy still diligently wrote hers onto cards like her mother had before her, which she kept in a plastic boxfile behind the sugar jar. Mrs Batts' card was right at the front. Above the various pencilled scribbles of colour concoctions and corresponding dates, she found what she was looking for. She knew the road. She walked along it twice a day on her way to and from work. It was almost opposite the house with the Noah's Ark in the garden.

She hung up her apron and tugged on a pair of tight black jeans, tucking her mini dress into the waistband. She shrugged on a calf-length black coat, turned up the collar and pulled a pair of black leather gloves from her pocket. She dragged her long dark hair back into a tight ponytail, lacquered it, exchanged her heels for pumps, then, gathering the tools of her trade into her shoulder bag, donned the gloves and slipped out the back way into the dusky alleyway, locking the door behind her.

That poor old lady. She had heard the story so often it had become a mantra. She had seen at it first hand within her own family: her father's affairs, his drinking, the pitiful excuses, the lies and finally the violence. And all because he had loved them in his own twisted, testosterone tempered way. And people wondered why she didn't want to play!

She waited for a hooded jogger to pass, then slipped silently through the garden gate and up the weed choked path to the Batts' front door, momentarily entertaining the notion that her evidence against Mr Batts was entirely circumstantial. She was doing to him exactly what Skye had done to his wife. It was her intuition talking. She hadn't actually been confided in. She peered through the letterbox into the stygian gloom of the suburban semi beyond. She could see no obvious signs of life downstairs and there were no lights on in the upstairs front bedroom. She sidled through the side gate and found herself at the back door. It was locked. Well, it was always worth a try. The only light at the back was beaming from a single naked bulb upstairs in what she thought of as the box room.

The houses were all the same in these roads: begun in the late thirties, but only finished after the war and with cheaper materials and less attention to detail than had originally been intended, touches of art deco mixed with make-do-and-mend. She shared one just like it with her mother only a few potting shed and bird table gardens behind this one. Her mother was rarely there of course, only showing up to collect her cut of the day's takings before gallivanting off with her latest man 'friend'.

Tracy pulled a hairpin from her pocket and deftly convinced the barrel lock that it was a key with the expertise of a professional cat burglar. The door opened with a sharp click and she stepped warily into what her mother would have referred to as the pantry. It was tidy enough, but odd, something she couldn't quite put her finger on. She moved through to the hallway, chancing a peek into the sitting room. This wasn't a couple's home. In fact, it wasn't very feminine at all. There were no ornaments or family photographs, no knick-knacks or keepsakes of any kind on show. The rooms were fastidiously tidy, but spartan.

Keeping herself tight to the wall in order to avoid any creaky boards, she made her way up the stairs, pausing just inside the stairwell to peer around the corner and through the open door of the box room. She had heard the distinctive clacking of an antiquated manual typewriter as she had climbed the stairs and could now make out the figure of a scruffy old man with his back to her, hunched over an old davenport desk, busily tapping away at the keys.

She checked her watch. It was a moment or two past five fifteen. Mrs Batts always had her hair done on a Wednesday at four on her way to her regular bingo session on the high street at five. If she was sticking to routine, albeit with a different hairdresser, then she wouldn't be home until seven. There was a familiar scent on the air as she stepped out onto the landing and slid her razor from its sheath. It was an old lady smell, or rather, it wasn't. It was that distinctive dry mustiness akin to mothballs, which she had always associated with old ladies. Mrs Batts had reeked of it more than most. She remembered as a girl smelling it on her mother's coat after a day in the salon, back in the day when husbands would collect their wives and drive them home, back when smoking was aloud in doors. She saw it now for what it was. Pipe smoke. Mr Batts was smoking a pipe, a smog cloud whirling in the light above his head like a ghostly grey halo. His hair was greasy and lank, as if it hadn't been touched for a fortnight. It hung over his tweed collar, curling toward the bottom and obviously artificially coloured. The vanity of men, she thought. How could a man of his age think that he could look anything but?

She stopped directly behind him, her head puncturing the smoke cloud like a ripper piercing a pea-souper and, in a single practiced movement, she slit his scrawny throat from ear to ear. He jolted upright in his chair, taken by surprise, his wrinkled hands instinctively grabbing at the wound in order to stem the torrent of blood that was now spilling onto his typewriter, his desk and the piles of paper around him.

She heard the gurgling splutter of his final attempt at speech: the sound that they had all made as their overly optimistic senses of self-preservation had battled to come to terms with their body's mortal predicament. He sputtered, he choked and he died. With the toe of her pump, Tracy pushed the corpse of her friend's dominator onto the floor.

As it fell, the head slipped against the rest of the body, sliding on the river of spilled blood and landing awkwardly, its startled face staring up at her. The face of her favourite client, Mrs Edna Batts, albeit with a chin full of silver stubble and minus her foundation.

Tracy gagged and bit the tip of her tongue, unable momentarily to make sense of what she was seeing.

Had they been twins? No. It wasn't that simple. Her brain struggled to accept what she really should have spotted years ago, something that Skye had said the first time she had seen her. Tracy had dismissed the idea, her mind refusing even to consider the possibility that Edna Batts, that sweet, sweet old lady, was really a man.

It was the hair that confirmed it. As she looked down at her grizzly handiwork she recognised her own signature. A good hairdresser can do that. Even after a fortnight's wear and tear, Tracy knew her own cut. Bile rose in her throat so fast that she didn't have time to pull away from the scene before relieving herself of her lunch. What had she done? She wasn't a killer. She didn't hurt innocents. She was a vigilante. She only hurt people who had wronged innocents. Tit-for-tat. An eye for an eye, like it said in the Bible!

But Mrs Batts was an innocent.

And now Mrs Batts was dead. She had killed her, him, no her! She had become that which she had been trying to destroy. She had become her father. She had become all those men who had wronged their wives. And worse than that. She had become Barry Ogilvy, the man that had been hassling her for a date since their last year at school, the man that she had reported to the police in the hope that he would take the rap for her crimes.

Her mind broke. She brought the blooded blade to her own neck and pulled sharply to the right.

24

The Life and Luck of the Great Dendini

Still the same, then, thought Dennis, pulling open his bedroom curtains with the much practised, melodramatic flourish of a fumble-fingered kid's entertainer flailing on the brink of irretrievable mojo failure at a six-year-old's birthday party and hoping beyond all reasonable expectation that the laws of the physical universe might be prepared to relent, just this once, and deliver him a tap-dancing white rabbit in a top hat and a spangly waistcoat to save his sorry arse from the inevitable trial by humiliation which was how these things usually ended. He hadn't known what he had expected to see out of his window that morning.

The even money was on exactly the same shit that had been out there eight hours earlier, only this time bathed in the dappled light of a cloud-shrouded sun or maybe dripping in shades of slimy grey as was more often the case.

But he could dream, couldn't he, he could hope? He had the right to wish for a better view onto a more hopeful future, didn't he? One morning he might whip back the ol' draylons to find blue waves lapping playfully against kissed golden sands, a beach towel laid just inches from the surf, bedecked with an as-near-as-dammit naked twenty-something temptress, oiling herself up whilst provocatively beckoning him to join her with her free hand.

And why the hell not? It was legal! And it happened to other people, apparently. Sometimes. Or at least, that was what he'd heard.

But no, not today, Dennis. There were no sexed-up beach-honeys in implausibly tiny lycra waiting to rub suntan lotion into the bits he couldn't reach, not today. There were only the two giant light-leaching gas storage tanks with their rusted steel gantry counterparts poised as if in permanent two-fingered mockery waiting to salute the arrival of yet another so-so day.

He sighed desperately and sat back down on the end of his bed. Hadn't he read somewhere that positive thought was all that was needed to exact positive change?

The power of affirmation and all that. Was that really true? Was your lot in life merely the result of how you envisaged yourself? Well, how much more desperate and affirming could he have been? Dennis snorted at the thought. It sounded a lot like alchemy to him. And although he crossed his fingers and held his breath every morning as he pulled on those curtains and whilst he closed his eyes and wished very hard every time he waved his magic wand over his top hat with the hidden compartment, he didn't really believe that anything exceptional might actually happen to him. And so, invariably it didn't. He wanted it to, though. He hoped that it would. But he didn't really believe that he deserved it to.

Maybe that was the problem, he worried.

But *why* didn't he deserve good things? He was a good man, he was good to animals and he'd never really done anyone any real harm. Alright, he came from modest stock, but should that completely preclude one the right to aspiration? No. Aspiration was what *drove* the lesser classes, it was what made them do the things they did which kept the wealthy, wealthy. Without the ordinary man's aspiration, society would've crumbled and died a long time ago!

As he walked down the stairs he saw the blurry outline of a burly figure, backlit by daylight behind the opaque glass panel beset into his front door. His heart jumped instinctively, convinced momentarily that someone had come to rob him. The letterbox suddenly clanged open and a pile of envelopes splattered onto the tattered old linoleum. Ah, postman, he realised, not a burglar then.

As he bent to retrieve his letters he heard that self-flagellating inner voice saying 'bills at best, notification of expulsion from the Magic Circle at worst'. So, what was the point in opening them, he thought? He'd just mentally jinxed any chance of an unexpected legacy falling into his less than worthy lap!

The rest of the day wasn't going to get any better either. He had a children's party at four.

The following morning Dennis walked toward his window with his eyes still tightly closed from a night's fitful and paranoid sleep, repeating the mantra 'I deserve, I deserve' as convincingly as he could, over in his head. He yanked back the curtains and opened his eyes and there before him . . .

. . . were the gas towers, flicking him the 'V's, just a little too smugly, he thought.

He sighed. And then he sighed again.

He sat down on the end of his bed. He tried to convince himself that he was actually a lucky man and that it could have been far far worse. At least he could see some sky between the towers. The bloke two doors down looked out onto the back wall of a factory.

All *he* could see was a flat brick wall with 'wish I was dead' graffiteed onto it at eyeline level.

And he wasn't in prison. That was also a plus, it had to be said. And alive surely had to be better than dead?

Perhaps . . . perhaps this was just how things were meant to be? Maybe this was the role that the universe needed him to play? He hadn't thought of it like that before. What if, he further considered, there really was no such thing as free will, what if everybody was just following a preordained script? What if choice was merely an illusion in the same way that he was able to make a child think that he'd just pulled a fifty pence piece from behind their ear? (Well, sometimes.) Surely that couldn't be right, though?

That would mean that for him to have any future luck to replace his current lacklustre existence then somebody else would inevitably have to suffer the consequences. Quid pro quo, and all that. Nah, he didn't believe that either. Positive thinking, Dennis, positive thinking. It might take a while, he told himself, but all good things came to those who waited. Hmmm.

The Great Dendini loathed children. He hadn't always felt that way, of course. Well, he wouldn't have set himself up in this business in the first place if he had hated them from the start, now would he? He had actually quite enjoyed their company at the beginning. It had been the naive wonder glinting in their sparkly kitten eyes whenever he had shown them something that, with their limited experience of the world, they had gladly perceived as magic. Truth be told, he was a crap magician, but back then, back before the technological revolution, kids had tended to be more trusting of adults and had been a much less discerning audience. Nowadays he was lucky if they could stay fixated for long enough for him to do his opening piece, the bit where he pulled a bunch of silk flowers from the lining of his magic cape to . . . snorts of derision, usually. They would be texting their mates or checking their emails on their smart phones or rifling through his pockets to 'see 'ow it's done'.

This day had started out no differently to any other. Gasworks in place, check. Bills on mat, double check.

He'd done the bunch of flowers, he'd done the coin from behind the birthday girl's ear, and he'd even done the endless knotted hanky routine with only two of the eight nodding off within the first five minutes. He had managed to rally the remaining six to reluctantly repeat his magic words, but just as he was about to lift off his hat to reveal Joey, his tired, fat and deaf white dove, he'd closed his eyes and wished really hard. Almost instantaneously he had felt a vicious peck from a bird's beak cutting right through his cheap hairpiece along with a tightening of a pair of talons much sharper than he knew Joey's to be. He whipped off his hat as he felt the blood begin to trickle between his eyes and suddenly the room erupted as all eight of his preschool conscripts screamed as a man and bolted for the door. The parents rushed in to find a bloodied Dennis brandishing a homemade wand in the face of seven large shrieking, pecking and shitting angry black ravens.

'. . . This is Peter Hunt for the BBC at the Tower of London with Raven Master Jack Higginbottom reporting on the disappearance of the Royal Ravens. Legend has it, Mr Higginbottom, that both the Tower and the Monarchy would fall if the Ravens ever left this spot. Is this likely, do you think?'

'I think that's utter bullsh—'

Dennis turned off his television and sat down at his kitchen table with his bandaged head in his hands. The police had finally released him, as the Queen had decided not to press charges.

The birds had been safely returned to the Tower and the media furore had died down. The parents who had booked him for the party had also taken pity on him and, having done really rather well out of the story themselves, had also agreed not to press charges. Dennis, however, had declined to be interviewed by the press. Well what could he have said? The Power of Positive Thought? Abracadabra did it?

He stood up and walked over to the oven, opened the door, knelt down in front of it and put his head inside. He reached up above and behind himself and switched on the gas. But instead of a stream of noxious fumes, his oven began to fill with what looked and tasted like seawater.

He withdrew and stood up, a thought having struck him as suddenly as had that raven's beak. He opened the back door and ducked as a seagull coasted in, dropping a still flapping fish into his hands.

'Come on in Dennis,' came a sultry voice from where his back yard had always stood, 'the water's lovely!'

So he didn't have any gas and neither would anybody else in the town, sadly. And the Monarchy was about to fall and who knew what else his recent change of fortunes might affect? But sod it, he might as well enjoy his new life even if everyone else had to suffer the consequences! Who knew how long it might last?

25

How Do I Feel?

I'm going to die.

It's going to happen, I know it is and there's nothing I can do to avoid it this time. I don't want to die, of course I don't, but Death has my number on quick dial and he may call at any moment.

But am I ready to die, yet? We all have to go some time, it's an inevitable consequence of life, but I've still got so much to give, y'know, I know I have, I just . . . need more time.

And when it happens, when that black-cloaked fiend finally comes a-knockin', which of its five foul faces will we see under that hood?

Will my end be accidental, will I slip from the curb and be run over by a number 47 bus that shouldn't even have been on that road, but due to gas main repairs along the usual route had been diverted at the last minute? So sad, a man snatched before his time, they'll lament, a poor soul who just happened to be in the wrong place at the wrong time, he who, but for fate's cruel twist, etcetera etcetera etcetera . . .

Maybe it'll be deliberate and I'll be stabbed through the heart in a moment of overstated revanchist madness by a spurned lover with a long-bladed kitchen knife and a notoriously short fuse? Will it be neither, could I possibly become the arbiter of my own sad demise? Overwrought by the guilt of my egoistic betrayal, is it possible that I might even hurl myself in front of that unexpected, but convenient bus or commit hari-kari in order to save my cuckolded love from the inevitable life sentence? Or will I be the victim of natural wastage, an unexpected illness or a sudden seizure? I could be one of the 'lucky ones', I suppose, who make it unimpaired through their three score years and ten, only to expire in my own bed at the grand old age of a hundred and ten, as shrivelled, incontinent and insensible as the day I was born.

But it's none of the above, as it turns out.

Apparently I'm scheduled for a slow, lingering death at the hands of a sadistic madman involving fetishistic torture and my pathetic whimpering that I be allowed to die quickly. Does that count as murder or assisted suicide, I wonder?

It'll play out over five nights, I'm told and it'll be a real Nielsen stormer, pushing the shows established pre-watershed censor rating to its very limit. Well, that's as maybe and who wouldn't want to go out in a blaze of primetime glory, possibly even heralded by a much feted Radio Times cover shot, but it is quite a final end, which means there'll be no chance of a Christmas cameo or even a full-time return later in the run after that bastard producer has moved on!

Now, I'm not the desperate ham that normally ends up in series like this, good God, no! I take my art seriously. I do my homework, I research the life that I'm about to take on. I absorb myself in every part that I play, literally becoming the character that's been written for me for the duration of the role. Even roles such as this—a shopkeeper in a twice-weekly soap with a hinted at, but as yet unrevealed mysterious past. I spent a fortnight stacking shelves in Tesco before I took that on, just to get a feel for the trade.

And I once slept rough for a month, beneath the arches, down beside the river in a cardboard box in order to gain the experience that I felt I'd needed to play a down-and-out in an episode of The Bill. Oh yes, I do the work! This technique is referred to in the business as 'Method' and it's a sacrifice that any actor worth their Equity card should be prepared to make, but sometimes . . .

Well, let's just say that going under a bus mightn't have been quite so glamorous, but it would certainly have been a less painful swansong. Obviously I would've spoken to a few road traffic accident survivors, visited a couple of A&Es to gawp at the less fortunate, maybe even have got my flatmate Tallulah to hit me gently with her Smart car in a controlled experiment in order that I might acquire the perfect facial expression for my final close-up, but ultimately the bulk of the scene would have been stolen by a stunt double—an 'athlete' rather than a thespian, in an unconvincing wig, mincing with the gait of a constipated Gerry Anderson puppet and trying too hard not to show 'face'.

At least this way I'll get to shine, I suppose. It can go on my showreel for my agent to hawk around the circuit. I might even get nominated for a BAFTA!

The director sent me down to the basement of Broadcasting House, to a room just beyond the sound recording studios for an appointment with a man whom she'd said could help me with my research material. He'd been eager to oblige me. Our meeting, she had explained, would be mutually beneficial.

Mr Foley is an expert in the field of coercing people into feeling a particular way at a particular moment while experiencing a television or radio programme. His work here for the BBC is extremely important, his dedication to duty: above and beyond, I am informed.

He introduced himself, shook my hand and then asked me to remove my clothes.

I never heard him say another word. He strapped my wrists to two heavy, rusty manacles that had been bolted to the rough brick wall above my head and then attached my ankles to two similar at skirting level, leaving me hanging in classic medieval torture position number one. He took his time preparing himself for his work: adjusting dials and switches on his equipment and then donning his plastic apron, half-mask and surgical gloves in front of me with all the ritualised relish of a Jeremy Kyle lie-detector reveal to a two-timing husband on daytime television. He took even longer to choose an implement with which to begin, but eventually settled on an iron poker which he'd had warming in a smouldering brazier in the far corner of the room. Then, with neither preamble nor warning he began prodding me, first in the stomach, then my side and then, as if saving the best till last, the souls of my feet. A red-hot poker. A red-hot poker! To say that I screamed would be like trying to describe the roar let out by a lion as whipped by a chair wielding ringmaster as a big miaow. As the wrenched muscles in my contorted face slowly reverted to factory settings, all bar a couple of spasming nerve endings that were still twitching in my left cheek, I tried to make a mental note of the facial shapes that I had pulled.

Mr Foley's next information gathering test brought the art of torture bang up-to-date as he clamped two industrial bulldog clips to my testicles and flicked a switch on the control box that the clips were married to by two curly red wires. I did my damnedest to remember the sequence of jerks, tics and gurns that followed and at which point I had started to froth, dribble and finally choke on my own strangled screams. There had been more pain to follow, much more, and at some point I must've blacked out. The last thing I remember was thinking that I was going to die.

And then I woke up to find myself propped up on a couch, a nurse tending to my wounds with an antiseptic swab. Of Mr Foley there was no sign.

'You actors do a wonderful job,' she said, affixing a plaster to my shaven chest. 'I don't think people realise what you lot put yourselves through for the benefit of your audience,' she went on. 'You really are society's true heroes, and don't let anyone tell you otherwise.'

I couldn't answer her. My mouth was stuffed full of cotton wool where I had lost a large tooth.

'And that Mr Foley,' she extolled, as she splinted my broken finger, 'he's a true legend, isn't he? A real slave to his art! His sound effects library is second to none!'

26

Rantiman

He's just been listening to a report on the radio that has been trying to convince him that the most stressful career path that anyone could choose to follow is that of a hairdresser.

Twaddle.

Apparently, research has shown that only one 'stylist' in five stays in the trade for longer than five years. And the excuse they invariably cite? Stress. Stress from having to stay cheerful all day long. because it's not an easy thing to be and nobody wants to have their hair cut by some whingey old cow with a voice like a Dalek and a face like a slapped arse. Frank feels that this says a lot about life in the twenty-first century. Frank isn't a cheery man by nature. He never has had much of a sense of humour and the disproportionate fury that he is now venting toward the programme's disembodied presenter would prove to anybody who may be listening that he doesn't have much of a sense of irony either.

Frank is in a hurry. This isn't unusual, Frank is always in a hurry. His career is far more important than that of a hairdresser and his rapidly thinning thatch and deeply scored face should be proof, if any is needed that it is also a lot more stressful. In fact, he makes a mental note as he sits for the third phasing of this particular set of traffic lights, that the next cheery person he sees, whether they look like a hairdresser or not, is going under his wheels. This makes him sound like a right old misery, but he isn't. He's a passionate man, he's just not a frivolous one and he takes his passions seriously. He has to, his passion is also his career. Like the train spotter who got a job driving trains, Frank has been lucky enough to land himself a job doing the one thing that he enjoys doing most in the world.

But he never expected it to be this stressful!

His psychiatrist thinks that he should lighten up a bit, take a break once in a while, try to 'employ perspective'. But his psychiatrist is a woman: she would say that. Women just don't understand the art.

His doctor prescribed him a course of anti-depressants, told him they were 'non-addictive', but how can something that de-stresses you momentarily not become addictive to a professionally stressed person?

A mate of a mate at his local sold him an eighth of marijuana, but all that did was to slow his reflexes and make him think that nothing in life could ever be that important.

So he's stuck with the stress. He's still looking for someone cheery to run over and he still hasn't moved an inch. The traffic around him is gridlocked. Nobody is going anywhere.

What's the matter with everyone? Haven't they got anything better to do with their time? Again the lights mock him in amber, telling him to get ready to go, and again the line in front of him hold their ground, unwilling, it would seem, to take a chance on what life might be like in the next road. Again he shouts a string of unfeasible suggestions toward his patronising nemesis. How is a gridlock even possible in a modern city where the lights can all be overridden remotely at the first sign of trouble? Where are the police? Isn't there some law that states that it is an offence to have a picnic on a yellow box junction?

It's almost two o'clock. He's never going to make it at this rate. He's getting cramp in his right leg where it's been hovering over the accelerator pedal for the past half an hour in readiness for a quick getaway. He's got a headache due to lack of oxygen to the brain as a result of the short shallow breaths he's been taking as he has got more and more wound up by his predicament. The background buzz of Radio 4 is replaced by the jangly jingle that always precedes a local traffic update. He learns that there has been an incident on Tottenham Court Road. Apparently some idiot has thrown himself off of the Centre Point tower and all the roads in the vicinity have been closed while the emergency services try to scrape up all the bits. Selfish bastard. 'And, no doubt they'll blame it all on stress,' he rants to nobody in particular, switching the radio off, lighting himself a cigarette and taking a long hard drag on it. He slams his free hand down hard against the steering wheel eliciting a sharp angry blast from his horn.

More profanities.

Two ten, and still he hasn't moved. He could walk. Why not just ditch the car and walk? It'd be quicker. His heart is racing, his head is racing, he's got a pain the length of his right arm. He's due on air in less than an hour and he can't even get a signal to warn them.

And suddenly he's moving. He's across the line, no longer governed by that soulless set of lights. He's in the box junction and his exit is . . . a car's length. That's all he is from the road he needs to be in, but he's stuck again. Why hadn't he dumped it while he had the chance? Now he's well and truly stuck. Forty minutes to go. What will they do if he doesn't show? What will the fans do? Today of all days. He can't let them down. He has a duty to perform.

The sweat is streaming from somewhere beyond his absent hairline, saltwater rock pools are forming in the gullies of his face. What will they do without him?

At five minutes to kick-off, still sat in his car straddling the box junction at Goodge Street, Frank suffers a massive and fatal stress related coronary. He is dead before his chin hits his chest.

Frank's radio is still playing thirty minutes later when the police arrive to remove his body. It's playing Frank's match: the one that he should have been providing the commentary for had he not just died on his way to the studio.

Frank would have taken the game a lot more seriously than his last-minute replacement is doing.

There's no passion to his delivery, no fevered excitement nor agonised despair, no over-egged anticipation and definitely no tears. In fact, there's no melody to the man's voice at all. He's taking it all in his stride. He's just watching the game and telling the listeners at home or at work or who might be trapped in their cars in a traffic jam somewhere what's going on on the pitch. It's a much easier listen. He's painting the scene. It's the difference between a Constable and Frank's Munck. Frank would have hated it, but then Frank would have hated the man anyway. Six weeks ago he was a hairdresser who just couldn't take the pace.

27

Seeing Things

Brian could not believe what he was seeing.

Not that he was particularly squeamish or anything, shit, no! He'd seen enough zombie action in his lifetime to turn an experienced mortician to the bottle, in his dreams, that was, he'd never actually seen a live zombie, or should that be 'dead' zombie? He could never be sure how that worked. And anyway, it didn't really matter as they didn't really exist, did they, did they? Brian wasn't all that sure of anything anymore. His life had never been what people called 'normal' and it was getting weirder by the day! The way things were going, he seriously doubted whether he'd have been all that surprised if he did actually see a zombie! No, the living dead he could cope with. He was used to having his nights haunted by the worm-ridden shambling remains of those whom he had loved and lost. It was the people who made them dead that he had issue with.

His heart was pounding, reverberating in his ears, and his throat was dry, parched like Saharan sand under a midday sun as it always got when he saw flashing blue lights in front of him. It was always the lights. It was what they signified: the Beginning of the End.

The blue light on this occasion was on top of a police car. It was parked outside that old florist bloke's on the hill, the one that Fleur had been wittering about for the past few weeks. Nasty piece of work, by her account. Wifebeater, apparently. There was an ambulance beside the police car, but its lights were off and from Brian's unfortunate wealth of experience in matters fatal, that confirmed one salient fact: somebody else was dead.

He hurried past the crime scene, keeping his face hidden beneath his hood and his pace steady, not wanting to draw attention to himself, hoping that the police at the gate would see nothing more than a fitness freak out for his morning jog. And that was all he was, right? He hadn't done anything and he definitely hadn't seen anything. He certainly hadn't seen Tracy Fenton sneaking through that same gate dressed all in black as he was jogging past last night. No. He most definitely hadn't seen that! His days of seeing things like that were long past. Be rational, Brian, he told himself: Tracy's a hairdresser, not a cat burglar or a murderer. It's just your mind playing tricks on you again, like it had done after . . . no! He wasn't going to open that box again! Zombies were one thing, but that . . .

His psychiatrist had explained it to him as a kid. It was a recognised condition. Attack victims often identified the first person on the scene after the event as their assailants, leading the person who had come to their aid to become the prime suspect. That's sort of what he was doing again now, he decided. He'd seen someone acting suspiciously and his fractious mind had transplanted a face that he knew for him. Yeah, that was it. It could've been anyone. So why Tracy? He didn't even know her that well. She was Fleur's boss: the shouty, man-hating manager of the salon . . . 'Stop it, Brian!' he told himself, it's not your problem, you know nothing. Keep jogging and try to think about something else. The game! Yeah. He had a game on Saturday. It was still just second team, but at least he wasn't on the bench this week.

He'd been hoping for a quiet life this time, but trouble always seemed to find him wherever they put him.

He'd grown up in care, the only survivor of an unsolved massacre that had claimed the lives of his entire family. At eighteen he had been the only witness to the gangland murder of his best friend which had necessitated his admission into the witness relocation programme. That was when he had become Malcolm. Before that he had been Sascha, but the police had decided that a name like that would have been too easy to trace. They'd given him a new nose as well, which he had thought had made him look more like his father, and relocated him up north. He'd liked it there. That's where he'd met Daisy and when she'd become pregnant he had moved into her parent's house and gained himself a proper family. For the first time in his life he had felt safe and secure. Of course, he still had the nightmares and he still sometimes thought he saw the faces of his dead family in crowds, but he could live with that. And the medication helped too. So long as he kept taking his tablets, everybody stayed dead. He'd got himself into the local team up there and had been about to play his first match when a renowned local villain had run down and killed Daisy and their daughter whilst the three of them had been out walking. The driver hadn't stopped, but 'Malcolm' and he had locked eyes, just for a second, but long enough for him to have been able to identify the culprit and put a notorious crook where he belonged.

They'd brought him back down south after that, pinned back his ears and dimpled his chin. He'd been expecting them to call him Michael this time, but they'd chosen Brian instead.

And so Brian had met Fleur when she'd been sick over his shoes in the queue for taxis outside Humpty's nightclub about a year ago. She'd reminded him of Daisy, in fact at first sight he'd thought that she had been Daisy, his mind playing those games with him as usual. He hadn't intended to let himself get close to anybody again. Experience had taught him that it'd all end in tears, but it had happened so quickly. He'd got himself accepted on an apprenticeship with the local team, Fleur had been given a pay rise and wham! In no time at all they had found themselves renting a little flat together at the cheap end of suburbia. It wasn't much, but at least he felt safe again. And Fleur was great, wasn't she? She didn't ask any awkward questions. So much of the world just went straight over her head that he could've probably moved someone else into the second bedroom and she wouldn't have batted a permanently tinted eyelid. The fact that he had no friends, no family and no past that he could speak of hadn't fazed her one iota. She hadn't seemed to have noticed that he hadn't brought any possessions with him, bar the clothes that he had been wearing at the time and she hadn't seemed at all perturbed about the monthly payments going into his account from an unlisted source. Fleur was perfect. Maybe this time he'd get it right? If only he could keep his mouth shut and his head down.

There was a lot that Brian hadn't noticed over the past few months . . .

It had started on the day that he'd arrived here. He had been sitting in the back of a taxi taking in the sights of his new home town when his driver had suddenly shouted 'Gotcha!' and run over a cyclist. As the cab had bumped all four wheels over the poor lady's broken body the driver had turned to Brian and begun to explain how 'the old witch had had it coming' and that 'the day of the pedestrian would soon be over'.

Brian had frozen. This had been the last thing that he'd needed! He had paid his fare and rejoined the pavement two roads later when he had been sure that he couldn't have been connected to the incident. A week later, whilst enjoying a coffee in the cafe on the high street, he had seen two dark-suited men on the roof of the building opposite push a grand piano from their perch, narrowly missing a stunned, but not altogether surprised passer-by by an anorexic gnat's whisker. And so had begun a highly improbable litany of muggings, burglaries and murders, the perpetrators of which he could easily have identified, had he been willing to swap this most precious shot at happiness for a social responsibility.

On a conscious level Brian had ignored them all, but somewhere deep within his psychosis, something was brewing. The zombies were massing.

He jogged steadily along the road, keeping his eyes ahead of him, but feeling the eyes of the policemen boring into his back. The criminal always returns to the scene of the crime, he remembered being told, there was every chance that he was at that point a lead suspect. When he reached the corner of St Kitt's Street he turned left, crossed the road and broke into a sprint to put some distance between himself and this latest moral dilemma. He cut into the alleyway that connected to the high street and ground to a sole strafing halt.

Zombies.

Was that . . . wasn't that . . . Daisy? He looked behind him and saw the reanimated corpse of the florist—Mr Batts, hadn't Fleur called him? And . . . wasn't that his mother behind Daisy? And . . . and that cyclist, the one that the taxi driver had killed. Well, why not? It was turning out to be that kind of a day! My dopamine levels must be off the scale, he thought, trying to remember whether or not he had taken his pills that morning.

'Malcolm,' croaked Daisy.

'Sascha,' croaked his mother.

'Brian,' rasped Mr Batts and the cyclist in unison.

Daisy's decaying body shuffled forward of the pack. He saw the imprint of a tyre tread across her face, exactly where he had expected to see it. Brian froze again. He knew he was imagining this, it couldn't really be what it appeared to be, could it? Surely he was finally going mad?

'You have to stop running, Malcolm,' Daisy croaked.

'You can't keep hiding, Sascha,' his mother rasped.

'You know what you saw,' Mr Batts gargled from just behind his left shoulder, blood bubbling from a fresh throat wound and splattering against Brian's ear.

'It's too much to keep in,' gurgled the cyclist, one lens slipping from her twisted spectacles and smashing on the pavement beside her.

'It'll eat away at your sanity, son,' drooled his long dead father, joining the party late through somebody's garden gate.

'For Fleur's sake,' crackled Daisy, her one unbroken arm

reaching out to him imploringly. 'You know what you saw. You know what you have to do.'

Brian/Malcolm/Sascha screwed up his eyes and slapped himself hard around the face.

'Dead stay dead!' he tried to convince himself, the way the psychiatrist had taught him. When he opened his eyes the zombies had gone.

He had to tell Fleur. Not about the zombies, well, not yet anyway (one bombshell at a time, eh?), but about Tracy. And about Mr Batts. And about Daisy and about his family and who had killed them. He had to tell her about Malcolm and Sascha and . . .

Brian ran as fast as his legs would carry him. He had to warn her. He knew what he'd seen: that look that he'd recognised on Tracy's face. He'd seen it before. He had tried to kid himself that it was his mind playing tricks, substituting faces like it had done so many times before, trying to make sense of the insane brutality of the world around him.

Little Sascha had known who had killed his family that night, all those years ago, he had always known.

'This is your big sister,' his father had told them one evening, just before his fourth birthday and it had confused his child's mind. He hadn't known where new sisters came from and he'd struggled to understand how a new sister could be older than both he and his brother. His mum and Dad had made a hamfisted attempt at explaining it to them, but he had never really taken it in. He had watched as Tracy had slit their throats and then that of his older brother, Nathan, and he had soiled himself as she had brought her blade toward him. But she had changed her mind at the last moment and had let him live on condition that he forget what he had seen.

So he had done. Until now. Just like he had taught himself to forget so many other things, his own name, even.

He turned the corner onto the high street and his heart sank. Blue lights. There was a police car parked on the pavement outside the salon. He was too late. All he had wanted was a quiet life. No thrills and no frills. He had no interest in other people and what they did or didn't get up to in the privacy of their own insanity, just as long as he didn't have to take part in it again.

He ignored the frantic pounding of his heart and the policeman who tried to stop him from entering the salon, sidestepping his outstretched arm like he would have done an opposing defender on the field, in order to reach Fleur, his ultimate goal.

'Brian?' Fleur queried, that trademarked look of dumbfounded incomprehension on her face, the same look that she employed whenever he suggested that they spend a Saturday night in. 'What you doin' 'ere?'

The plod had taken in the situation and, given Brian's size relative to his own, had decided to let him stay. Brian grabbed his girlfriend with both overdeveloped arms and hugged her delicate body to him.

'It's Tracy,' he began, but she cut across him, extricating herself from his manic embrace.

'Oh, I know! Awful, innit! Tha's her mum over there,' and Brian turned to take in the original Mrs Fenton in profile, sobbing against the PC. 'They think she killed 'erself,' she explained.

Now it was Brian's turn to frown.

'Looks like she killed Mr Batts and then did 'erself. Weird. Don't make sense does it?'

It didn't make any sense to Brian either, but then Tracy never had done. She had killed his family in front of him when she had only just met them. He would never know why. And, according to the tittle-tattle that his radar was picking up from the twittering girls in the corner, she may well have murdered a lot of other people too. But what made even less sense to him now was what he had come here to do in the first place.

The telephone rang on the reception desk and Fleur moved away to answer it, giving him a moment alone to think. Brian couldn't help but stare at Mrs Fenton. Pieces were falling into place in his mind. She must have been married to his father before he had married his mother, long before he and Nathan. Had he left Tracy and her mother for that sweet Jamaican dancer that he missed so much? Had that been the tipping point for Tracy? Who would ever know now? It felt, however, that a huge grey cloud had lifted from the fogged miasma that had served as his mind.

He took a final look at the grieving mother who probably had no idea of the extent of her daughter's crimes. Part of him wanted to tell her, needed to tell her, even, to finally get it off his chest, but what would have been the point in that? What did he have to gain by telling anybody anything now? Sod the zombies. What did they know anyway? Probably better if he took a leaf out of Fleur's book and tried not to notice the things that didn't affect him.

Time to stop looking for trouble, he decided.

And definitely time to stop seeing things.

28

Other People

Ali was an extremist, or at least, that's what other people called him. 'Other People', tsk! What did they know? It was because of other people that he did what he did! It was because of other people that he was up here now: sitting on this ledge, one floor down from the top of Burj Khalifa, at 2,723 feet still the tallest building in the world, well, until the Americans completed their 'Freedom Tower', or whatever it ended up being called. He'd already decided that that was going to be his next target, though right at this moment he was trying not to think about that. He was trying not to think about heights at all.

Extremist Ali, that's what the press called him.

He'd have preferred something more heroic, a title more befitting of his courageous daring. A superhero name, maybe? How about . . . 'Action Ali'? Or 'Danger Man Ali', no wait, that one was already taken, wasn't it? How about simply 'God' then, because that's how it usually made him feel. (Usually.) Powerful. So bloody powerful. Just for those few moments. He was doing something that very few others would ever dare to do and he was doing it all for a noble and worthy cause. Yeah, some days he felt like a god, but hey, what was wrong with that?

He laughed as that thought flittered through his mind. He was currently trying so desperately not to look down, his quick bitten fingernails attempting to gouge grooves into the smooth concrete of the ledge, the evening breeze whipping at his dangling ankles.

Other people. Other bloody people.

He'd been born with a disability, though not one that was recognised by the medical profession. He had been born with a total absence of charisma. He was the one that people didn't notice, the kid whose name the teachers forgot, the boy who never got picked for the team and who didn't spring to mind when mothers were writing out party invitations. The child who got left behind on the school trip to the zoo because nobody had remembered to count him.

It was probably inevitable then, that he would one day try to reinvent himself in something of an extreme way in order to redress the humiliating imbalance of his formative years. That was when weedy little Alistair Harley had become Extremist Ali.

Well, at least they noticed him now, even if they had given him a name that made him sound like some bomb-toting crackpot jihadist!

It had all begun in his teens when a sudden surge of hormones had necessitated extreme measures to ensure that he got noticed by the opposite sex. What had started as a series of death-defying stunts on a BMX bike had soon escalated to scaling the outsides of tall buildings and then eventually to throwing himself off of the top of tall buildings with a parachute or a glider strapped to his back. They soon noticed him then! He claimed to 'know no fear', that was his sexy strapline, and as he was putting his life on the line for charities, his stupidity was usually considered heroic. (Cue the wholesale removal of lingerie on an international scale.)

'KNF!' He would shout for the ladies and the cameras alike, as he ran toward the edge of any suicidally high plateau: 'Know No Fear!' And the truth was that he didn't, not whilst other people were watching him, anyway, not while the adrenaline was pumping through his veins, not whilst he could hear his name being chanted like a mantra for being the greatest base jumper in the world!

But take away the adulation: Ali's class A drug of choice, his all-numbing addiction to public acknowledgement and recognition for his unique (if a little pointless) talent and you'll find that same shy little boy who got left at the zoo gates because he was too scared to speak up for himself in front of other people.

Ali had come out onto this ledge so that he could have a quiet look at the view before tomorrow's planned jump.

It always helped with the confidence on the day if he felt that he knew what he was leaping into, though he was well aware that it made little or no real difference in the mad scheme of things. He felt that it looked better for the cameras if the whole ridiculous charade appeared carefree and spontaneous. It wasn't, of course; it was meticulously planned, right down to the tiniest of details.

Ali didn't really like heights. He'd always thought that was because he was a short bloke and for a short bloke everything was either a long way up or a long way down. He had often blamed his shortness for his childhood insignificance and so conquering heights, at least publicly, had been a big thing for him psychologically. It was all part of his public persona: the big man. The big man who jumped off big things.

The big man who jumped off big things fearlessly.

Yeah, right!

He hadn't told anybody that he had arrived early for a final recce, he never did, so nobody had known that he had been out there on the ledge looking down on the glittering lights of a hot Dubai night. It was all a part of his ritual, you see. He needed to be alone, invisible to all but the stage that he was about to step onto: respecting the void, like an actor blocking his movements and taking possession of an auditorium the night before the opening. It was an essential part of the show to Ali. Before he could present himself in front of 'Other People', to be a part of their crazy, egocentric world, he had to centre himself, to be at one with his own insignificant universe, to wrest control of the situation from those who pulled his strings. For once he was in free fall he would be the big man and nobody would be able to ignore him!

He had been taking in the view of the bay where he intended to land when he heard the door behind him being closed and locked from the inside. He turned quickly, searching for a handle that wasn't there. He hammered on the toughened glass of the window, but nobody heard him. Everybody had gone home for the night.

He was just a little man on top of a tall building that nobody could see or hear screaming, longing for the company . . . of Other People.

29

Mystery's

And she thinks that's erotic, does she? Well, I suppose it all depends on which angle you're coming at it from, don't it? Personally I find it about as much of a turn-on as unwrapping a packet of hobnobs, less so if there's chocolate involved. And it's not just because it's the only trick she's got and that I've had to endure that same trick every night for the past five years, no. Granted, that doesn't help, but that's not the real bugbear with Coco. It's her total lack of passion that gets me, the emptiness: like she's showing me a pornographic photo of herself with the same indifference I'd expect had she shown me a picture of her grandmother, that burned out, 'girl in a coma' act that these people just seem to lap up. She calls it burlesque, striptease, to the commoner: the clue is in the job description, luv, titillation. I should be willing her to go further, further and faster. Well I am, the latter, but only because I've got a bus to catch.

Why am I watching at all? Because it's my job, that's why. Hi, I'm Elvis and this is my club. Ordinarily I'd be in the back office right about now, counting the evening's door receipts, but for the past few nights Terry the thong-catcher has been laid up with flu, so I've been doubling as front of house. I know what you're thinking: collecting up the laundry, that's not a fitting job for the owner of such a classy establishment, but I don't see it like that. To me it's more a case of asset management. That lingerie don't come cheap, y'know and if one of our punters were to pocket a wayward basque or a stray suspender belt, well then, that's going to impact on my night's profits, ain't it?

So I stands here at the side of the stage, watching Coco take off her clothes, for all the world like Dara the doorman has his knife to her throat, and I make a mental note to remember where she threw what and at whom so I can safely retrieve said sweaty garment once she's shuffled back to her kennel.

It wasn't always like this, here though, oh no. This place, it used to have a very different reputation.

We had everybody in here back when, all the names: they all came to Mystery's, oh yes! Singers, comedians, poets, oh, we had 'em all. I look at Coco with her kohled, dead eyes and I think back to those days now, those glorious days, when people expected more from their arts, back when people were looking for stimulation rather than simulation, back when entertainment meant something more than the flash of a crackhead's tattooed arsecrack.

But I'm being unfair, unfair to Coco and unfair on the punters. I check myself as one of her stockings slaps me in the face, jolting me back to the reality of the here and now. I've got a business to run. That means getting punters through the door on a nightly basis and fleecin' 'em with drinks on a 150 per cent mark up.

If I have to watch this emaciated, libido-sapping, titless wonder every night for the rest of my days to do that, then so be it. There're worse ways to make a living, I s'pose.

But it used to be so much more fulfilling, y'know?

The trouble with artists, though, is that they feel too much.

Ha! I used to think they was acting: all that heart wrenching, tortured soul business, I thought it was all a play! I thought those guys were somethin' special, somethin' I could never be. Ha! I had this naive mental image of the poet and the lyricist and the observational comic, sitting at their typewriters by day, surrounded by books and old films, tapping into the great gestalt of human emotion while drinking mug after chipped mug's worth of neat caffeine with heaped sugar as the ashtrays overflow and the screwed-up balls of discarded paper grow ever higher 'round their ankles. I saw the singers spending long hours staring into brightly-lit mirrors, searching for the perfect expression to match the correct level of soul-rending torment in those finely crafted words. I saw ephemeral beings of light and shade, shining stars with the supernatural powers to transport the average punter with their average earnings and their average lives to the dizzy heights and the desperate lows that they might never have otherwise experienced for themselves.

Well, they were special alright.

Turns out just not in the way I'd imagined!

Dara's got some bloke in a discreet half-nelson and is escorting him towards the service entrance for making a pissed-up lunge for Coco's crotch whilst I was dreaming. He missed, of course. She might look like a slow night at the morgue, but where an inebriated half-arsed grope's concerned, she has an uncannily keen spidey sense.

Special, yeah, they were definitely special, special in that way that psychopaths are special, as in 'something ain't quite right' special. Special as in all that 'feel my pain' shit—that ain't an act, oh no! That ain't 'Method', that's the real deal. That's life mimicking art and who wants to pay for that?

She's down to the thong now and I've got the place staked out. I know where every last piece of wardrobe fell and I saw the guy who pocketed her other stocking. By rights, and by that I mean the laws of nature, I ought to be stirring by now, but I'm not. Y'know, the first time I noticed this lack of . . . stimulation, I thought I might be turning to the dark side, but no, everything's in proper working order down there, she just don't do it for me. The artists, yeah, they did it for me. They reeled me in, they suckered me and bled me until I found 'em out, till I realised the trick they was tryin' t'pull!

There goes the thong, now and up goes the cheer. That's all you're getting, lads: a quick flash of what makes her a her and she's off, quicker than she's managed anything all night.

There she was, for the briefest flicker (blink and you'll miss it), alone, naked in a roomful of middle-aged . . . bankers and the like. You wouldn't think she'd be able to hide anything in that state, would you? But, y'know, I've been watching her all this time and I realise somethin'—I know absolutely nothing about her. Naked, but wrapped so impenetrably inside that vulnerable chalk-white skin like it's a suit a' bleedin' goth armour.

Clever. When she walks out of here she can just melt into that ever flowing torrent of ordinary people, disappear like she never was and none of these guys, none of 'em, would recognise her again if she served them up their dinner when they got home.

That was the thing about artists, see. Up there in their sequins and their silks, never more than a flash of stockinged thigh and then . . .

. . . then they go an' open their bleedin' mouths.

That's where it all falls apart for me, see? What is it that keeps a place like this profitable in the midst of a double-dip recession? Escapism, that's what. People come here lookin' for some relief from the reality of their pointless existences. Now, they could just buy themselves a bottle of cheap supermarket vodka, score themselves a packet of white powder from round the back of that same supermarket and blot out the world in front of X Factor in the squalor of their own homes *or* they could come here to Mystery's, where our team of highly talented turns an' troubadours could whisk them away into the realms of fantasy with a cocktail of humorous tales, romantic lyricism, easy charm and poetic imagery, now that's what I call entertainment!

But have you ever met an actual artiste? You think *you've* got troubles, bud?

We advertised it as 'Cabaret Night', but we may have done better just to've called it 'Group Therapy' and been done with it. 'Damaged Goods' is how I see 'em now. These people weren't faking it and they weren't about to go quietly, either. Talk about 'hearts on their sleeves', these guys had had their hearts ripped out and stapled to their foreheads! Not pretty. No . . . mystery.

And that's not what people want to see, right? They want heightened reality, they want a fiction: somewhere to hide for a moment from the noise of the world. They don't want to know the inner workings of a stranger's soul, they want adventure. They don't want to know what drove them to it, they've got enough of that shit in their own living rooms.

Coco's fumbling with a fresh pair of knickers as I step backstage and dump my pile of nylon and satin onto the dressing table beside her. It's just me and her now. She smiles her sad, faraway smile as she steps into her clean underwear and slowly pulls them up. She doesn't speak and she doesn't turn away as I watch her redress.

I've seen her all and from so many angles, but yet I've seen nothing. I don't even know her real name. And I don't want to know it, either. Because once you know too much about a person, once there's no longer any mystery to be pondered . . .

. . . then what have we got?

'Same time tomorrow, then?' I ask, as she zips up her anorak and picks up her shopping bags.

She just smiles and heads out into the night.

30

Where Have All the Hysterical Housewives Gone?

There were any number of inherent risks to be considered in his line of work, but Ernest had understood that from the outset. It was a dangerous profession to be a part of and perhaps more so these days than ever before. Every hour of his working life saw the potential of exposure to an unlimited variety of debilitating and even fatal diseases, viruses and infections, many of which were incurable and were easily transmittable within the confined space in which he spent most of his working day. One would clearly have had to have been clinically insane or suffering from some perverse sexual fetish for the near-death experience to have considered taking on the role, but Ernest had been neither.

It was a job, someone had to do it, and you got paid shitloads of money for the inconvenience. And there were plenty of perks too, let's not forget that. As a respected member of the community, nay, one of the four pillars of any civilised society, one gained an automatic air of trust and respectability and even a degree of fame in one's locale, if that was one's particular bent, though Ernest had always been adamant that this had not been a contributing factor to his decision to become a doctor. Then there were the presents from satisfied patients, invites to civic soirees and society dos, applications to join private members clubs rubberstamped as soon as their secretaries saw the initials 'Dr' prefixing his name. And there were also the opportunities to prostitute one's signature for twenty quid a throw on a passport application or whenever a will needed witnessing.

Oh, yes there were perks, alright. And of course, long-term exposure to the various maladies of the ordinary man did tend to render one somewhat immune to said afflictions, so, all in all, when he weighed the pros and cons of his chosen vocation, Ernest had always felt that he'd been on to a pretty good screw.

But whilst his younger, less entrenched self may have fretted unnecessarily over the possible threats to his physical wellbeing, he had naively spared no conscious concern for the likelihood that his mental health may also have been in the firing line from his unexpectedly frequent exposure to the 'less than' ordinary man (or woman).

Dr Ernest Sorbet had chosen this particular practice because its retiring senior practitioner, a member of his golf club, had told him that it was a quiet suburban patch where his most common task would be the repeat prescribing of valium to middle-class housewives in order to help them to deal with their white-collar husbands' secretarial indiscretions. That had been twenty-five years ago. Oh, how the world can change over a quarter of a century! The valium pills had been superseded by Prozac: a more effective mid-term mind number, that was also reputed to be less addictive than its forebear. Its proscription, though, was more tightly controlled, as were the definitions of the disorders that it could be dispensed for. Life had been so much easier back in the eighties, when everybody just suffered from 'stress'. These days everybody felt the need to suffer from a 'condition', which added an undue amount of stress to a doctor's workload. Ernest was a GP, a general practitioner, which meant that he knew a little about a lot, but not a lot about very much.

His job was to listen to his patient's problems and decide whether: (a) they were on the fiddle, (b) they could be numbed and pacified with high commission repeat prescription drugs, or (c) be referred on to an expert. He was a buffer, a middleman, a cog in a machine, yes, that was what it all boiled down to these days: filing reports and making recommendations, deciding how best to allocate the surgery's meagre budget—another box of happy pills for Angie Fenton and a word in Miss Featherstone's ear about not being so accommodating with appointments for the likes of Barry Ogilvy. Hmm . . . and hadn't that been where it had all started to go wrong: an innocent misdiagnosis due to stress on his part? Barry had told him what he was going to do. He'd told him about the voices, whispering to him in the night, filling his head with paranoid delusions about people whom he barely knew.

'Fob him off,' he'd told Miss Featherstone. 'Tell him what you tell all the patient's whom you don't know socially, that I can't fit him in for at least four weeks. He's a timewaster, he's making it up, he's just after a sick note.'

Miss Featherstone hadn't needed to be asked twice.

But now, sadly Miss Featherstone was gone, murdered in cold blood, murdered by Barry Ogilvy along with Ernest's favourite chemist and two other innocent bystanders, all because he hadn't taken his psychosis seriously.

It had been a blow to his reputation, certainly and the press had had a field day, of course.

So he had taken some time out—a sabbatical was how it had been worded for his patients on the waiting room noticeboard. Compassionate leave, it had said on his record, to help him to get over the stress of his receptionist's death. They had, after all, been friends for a very long time.

Ernest had been different when he'd returned to work. He had spent three months in a retreat in North Wales, learning to live off the land, baking bread and making peace with his battlefield of a conscience.

It had been a mistake that anybody could have made, he had

taught himself to reason, and one that in the fullness of time would doubtless be forgotten, provided he didn't make any similar mistakes in the near future.

On the inside, however the damage had been done, his confidence had been compromised, but he wouldn't let that show, no, he wouldn't let that show. He was a professional.

He'd been doling out the pills for long enough to know how to make someone appear calm and collected on the surface when in reality they were as mad as a box of frogs. He'd been doing that his whole career. Ernest knew the cocktail and the dosages that would on the one hand numb the constant pain while at the same time heighten his senses to a near superhuman degree. He had never felt so good, so clearheaded, so . . . vital! It was time to stop being a middleman and get on with some proper doctoring, to start looking at his treatments in more of a holistic way. He would be better than ever!

But what was it about this town? Where had all the hysterical housewives gone?

Were they putting something in the water around here? The whole town seemed to have gone bonkers overnight!

There was Mr Vartes insisting that he'd evolved into some kind of God-being. Mr Batts: a man of seventy-eight, demanding a sex change on the NHS. Mr Goodman: convinced he was being stalked by government agents and a sudden plethora of weeping widows all certain that the town had its own serial killer. And that wasn't including that poor boy with the zombie fixation! How was he supposed to deal with patients like that? Perhaps they'd always been there, Miss Featherstone's much missed receptioning system having filtered them out for him?

Ernest longed for the old days, when 'pull yourself together, dear' was an acceptable treatment. He fished around in his draw for that nondescript bottle of pills that the obliging new chemist had given him in exchange for a reference to the lodge. He unscrewed the cap, poured a generous grouping of small red pills into his palm, popped them into his mouth and washed them down with a full can of caffeinated energy drink. He pulled up the file pertaining to his next patient and skimmed through it. Dennis Trout, 48, children's entertainer. Hmm . . . believes he really can do magic.

The one who let a flock of ravens loose at a kid's birthday party so that they'd take his act seriously. He poured another few pills straight down his throat.

Cut out the middleman, he thought. Treat the problem, not just the symptoms. Or better still: cut out the middleman—sod the patients, treat the doctor instead!

Other titles from Desert Hearts & RRRANTS:

Quaking in Me Stackheels

A Beginner's Guide to Surviving Your First Public Performance

Paul Eccentric

Have you got what it takes to stand up on a stage in front of a sea of expectant strangers and wow them with your pearls of wit and wisdom or are you too scared of what might happen to you if the crowd suddenly turned ugly? Remember, there are more of them than there are of you and they know who you are! Have you ever wanted to know how to control an audience or to put a heckler in their place? Would you know how to prepare your show for maximum audience impact? And what exactly do you know about microphone technique and presentation? If you are a singer, a poet, a comedian or a public speaker of any kind; or if you would just like to know how to appear more confident in company than you naturally feel, then let Paul Eccentric, performance poet, singer, stage director, compere and all-round show-off, talk you through the tricks of the trade, learned the hard way over his 25-year career stomping the boards in big boots... Invaluable lessons for any would-be performer!

Paul Eccentric is a poet, novelist, singer, lyricist, playwright and director. He has also been coaching performers in the art of confidence and surviving their first night since 2009. Among his various musical forays into the worlds of jazz, punk, polka, skiffle, swing and doowop, Paul has both written and sung for The Odd Eccentric since 1984 and The Senti-Mentals since 1998. He has published two solo poetry collections Lyrical Quibble & Quip and The Kult of the Kazoo, and a novel Down Among the Ordinaries. As one half of The Antipoet he has released two beat poetry CDs, Tights Not Stockings and Hanging with Poets. His most recent albums Odds 'n Sods and Who Knows, Who Cares? are available from Doopop Records.

www.deserthearts.com
www.rrrants.co.uk

Other titles from Desert Hearts:

Destinations
David R. Morgan

"DESTINATIONS is the arrival of the most complete collection of my writing ever, from brand-new poems and prose-poems to some that have been published before. I write to try to make sense of things, wondering what Dark Matter is, why the galaxies are speeding faster and faster away from each other, why we live and why we die, why pigs aren't green and grass doesn't go oink. So read this book with its unexpected twists and turns, meet my parents, children, werewolves, angels, ghosts, aliens and estate agents – it's one hell of a journey!"

The Commuter's Tale
Oliver Gozzard

Inspired by the spirit of Lord Byron, a careworn commuter abandons his humdrum life to embark on a voyage of adventure with a rapper he meets on the train. A swashbuckling thriller in verse, penned by an exciting new writing talent! **What the experts say: 'The Commuter's Tale is Belloc meets Byron meets Chaucer'(Attila the Stockbroker), 'A rollicking odyssey of joy' (Radio 4 poet Elvis McGonagall), 'I just couldn't do it justice!'(Jeremy Paxman)**

The Little Big Woman Book
Llewella Gideon

Forced into temping hell, out-of-work actress Cynthia Cynical embarks on a wickedly comic guided tour of her office and the characters that inhabit it. The Little Big Woman Book takes a humorous look at life, love and rites of passage for the Black thirtysomething woman in Britain today. Inspired by the hit Wet End stage show and BBC Radio 4 series by comic actress and writer Llewella Gideon, best known for her work in shows like The Real McCoy, Absolutely Fabulous, Murder Most Horrid and the Spice World: The Movie.

www.deserthearts.com